The Speed of Wind

Sara Jo Easton

© Sara Melissa Miller 2012

All rights reserved. No part of this book may be reproduced in any form or by any electronic or mechanical means without permission in writing by the author, except by a reviewer, who may quote brief passages in a review.

This is a work of fiction. Names, characters, businesses, organizations and places and events are either from the author's imagination or used fictitiously. Any resemblance to actual persons, living or dead, events or locations is completely coincidental and, in the author's opinion, incredibly bizarre.

For my second love, wherever he may be.

Prologue,
Or A Tale the Onizards Tell Their Children When The Rain Falls

The Great Lord of the Sky created all Onizards and humans as equals, but he gave them different abilities to suit their spirits. Some Onizards were granted the power to attack their enemies with fire; others were given the power of the earth to heal. Some were given the power to attack with a jet stream of water from their mouth, and still others were made like the wind, the swiftest of all creatures. For a time, the Onizards did not understand that their differences made them stronger, and they simply identified themselves as Children of the element they were blessed with. It would take a great sacrifice to unite the Onizards; Senbralfi, son of the Fire Chieftain, jumped in front of his own kinsman's blast to save the daughter of the Water Chieftain, and suffered burns that should have killed him. But Senbralfi did not die; the Great Lord of the Sky saw how much Senbralfi loved, and because of that love Senbralfi became the first Leyrkan of the Sandleyr, Senbralni.

When the Great Leyrkan Senbralni left this world for the sky, the precious light that he carried with him did not leave the world. Most of it went to his four children, who also inherited his powers of ultimate empathy. Two of them chose to rule during the day, when they could see their father in the sky, and the other two chose to rule during the night. They became known as the Children of Light, for all knew of the precious gift and burden they carried for the world. They took care of this light well, passing it on to their chosen heirs when they died. The Day Kingdom's heirs did not appear as concerned with bloodlines as the Night Kingdom's heirs; Senbralni's descendants continued ruling during the night in an unbroken chain from parent to child, until it was said by many that Senbralni's bloodline was destined to rule the Night Kingdom.

But not all of the light in the world went to Senbralni's children. Every creature in the world was given the gift of light. Not all had the same amount of light; some turned away from this gift and became demons, scorning life and love. They caused the great pain in the world, pain that caused the Children of Light to cry whenever they felt it. One of the most noted demons in Sandleyr history was Deybralfi, called Fire Queen. She killed her own mother, Leyrque Ammasan of the Day Kingdom, and for ten years after this murder, there was only one Child of Light in the Day Kingdom. The Fire Queen took control of the Sandleyr, claiming it was her right as daughter of the former Leyrque. All creatures of the Sandleyr suffered greatly under the rule of the Fire Queen; many humans lost their lives to the Fire Queen's frequent rages, and the Onizards were forced to live lives of fear.

But some beings embraced their gift of light and learned to love all of the Great Lord of the Sky's creations. In this time of strife, Jena the human became Bond of Senraeno, son of Lady Rulsaesan of the Day Kingdom. The lowly non-nature Teltrena, in her noble efforts to protect the young Onizard Senraeno and his human Bond Jena, became the Lady Teltresan of Day and ended the oppressive reign of the demon Fire Queen. When she became the joinmate of Delbralfi, son of Leyrkan Mekanni and Lady Delsenni of the Night Kingdom, many looked to her to continue the line of Senbralni, though she could never be a member of the Night Kingdom.

Idenno, the brother of Mekanni, became a powerful Child of Water through his frequent rain dance exercises. Though Leyrque Rulsaesan freed him from the duties of Watchzard, he continued to watch over the Sandleyr, waiting for an old enemy to strike. For six years, he and his namesake Deldenno trained for the turmoil they knew would come. The Fire Queen would never give up a chance for revenge, and she would not die from a simple exile to the wilderness. It was only a matter of time before the Children of Light would need champions, both old and new, to protect the fragile peace of the Sandleyr.

Chapter 1

Uncle Iden, why is there smoke on the horizon?

Idenno lifted his head, staring in the direction his namesake Deldenno was concentrating on with unusual attention. It had been six years since Deldenno's birth, and as he grew to adulthood he had changed from a child hungry for learning to a wise and trusted friend. It was strange how quickly the lad had grown to be an adult Onizard taller than his elder, but he still had some appearance of youth, and that was enough for Idenno. He would only start feeling old when Deldenno's dark blue skin became pale with age.

The aging process was not a real concern for Idenno now. There was definitely smoke on the horizon; the black cloud rose over the treetops, above even the giant pillar with a partially destroyed bowl at the top that was the Leyr Grounds, the place where all Onizard eggs were kept. Idenno's thin cerulean body had been covering the rock formerly reserved for Watchzards, but now he stood up on it to get a better look at the smoke.

I do not know, Delden, but it worries me, he said with the telepathic speech of the Onizards.

You don't think Erfasfi is up to some sort of prank, do you? Delden asked as he stepped closer to the edge of the woods that surrounded the Sandleyr.

Idenno could not resist the urge to smile. *With that kind of smoke rising, it looks like far too large of a fire to be a prank, and I don't think Delbralfi's son is capable of that much mischief with his brother keeping him in line.*

Besides, I'm here, said a pale orange Child of Fire as he flew out of the Sandleyr entrance. His impish smile did not match his narrowed brown eyes until he noticed the true topic of conversation. *Wow, what an awesome smoke cloud!*

Erfasfi, show some consideration for whatever might be vanishing with that smoke, said a dark grey Child of Wind as he followed the Child of Fire. His large green eyes seemed out of place on his short, thin body, but Idenno had to assume large eyes were useful for spotting danger when a Child of Wind was using his powers of speed. With the enthusiasm only a brotherly rivalry could bring, the Child of Wind zoomed ahead of Erfasfi as soon as he was out of the narrow entrance. Within an eye blink, he was near Idenno.

That's not fair, Xoltorble! Erfasfi shouted when he realized what his brother had done. *You promised not to use your powers like that!*

You promised not to call me Xoltorble! I'm Xolt; I don't need that fancy name Mom gave me.

And I'm Deybralfi the Fire Queen. I don't like my real name, so I force everyone to use a nickname I made up!

Shut up, Erfasfi! It's wrong to joke about things like that! Xolt said, his eyes widening at the mention of the terrible monster from his mother's stories.

Why do you have to be so negative, Xoltorble?

Why do I have to be the brother of an idiot? Xolt whined.

Boys, please! Idenno shouted, causing the two younger Onizards to fall silent. *The Fire Queen is not a joke. Honestly, I'd never expect such immaturity from boys nearly two years old!*

Erfasfi's the immature one, Xolt explained, glaring in his brother's direction.

Silence! Deldenno exclaimed. *Listen, all of you.*

Iden gave the boys a stern look of disapproval before he noted how grim Deldenno seemed. After Idenno stepped toward his namesake and listened for a few moments, he understood the reason for concern. Screams were coming from the direction of the smoke.

Is Grandpa Mek sick again? Xoltorble asked after they had all stood listening for a few moments.

I wish that was all it was, Idenno said. *Delden, watch Erfasfi and Xoltorble while I figure out what's going on. I don't want them doing anything rash.*

Uncle Iden, if there is a fire that bad, it will take more than one Child of Water to get rid of it. You'll need my help.

If it is a fire that bad, those two should not be anywhere near it.

Excuse me, sirs. I can help, said a female voice, wavering slightly as if the speaker was incredibly shy.

Idenno turned quickly and saw a Child of Earth standing near Deldenno. If the boys had not been watching, he probably would have jumped from the sheer shock. How had she managed to sneak up on him, when he had once been Watchzard? He should have been able to notice a dark green Onizard taller than him, especially with the way her brown eyes sparkled as she looked at Deldenno. He thought he recognized her from somewhere, but he could not place her. *When did Teltresan teach you how to startle me like that?*

She didn't, the Child of Earth said as she shrugged. *I just wanted to breathe the fresh air, but apparently it doesn't exist at the moment. I'll make sure these two don't run off while you two strong Children of Water put a stop to the fire. Call for me if you need help with any injuries!*

Fine, said Deldenno as he tore his eyes away from her. *Come, Uncle Iden, we haven't got any time to spare!*

As Deldenno ran to the forest path, Idenno noted a strange look on the Child of Earth's face that seemed almost like she was trying to hide some sort of disappointment. Then he shrugged and followed Delden. No need to worry about odd Onizards until the serious problem of the fire was solved.

Chapter 2

Deldenno ran down the forest path, trying to keep his thoughts away from pretty Children of Earth. But with the trees partially obscuring the smoke cloud, he could not help but let his thoughts drift as he ran. Why did the smoke cloud have to show up now, at all times? Then again, he could hardly curse the smoke cloud when he hadn't exactly been diligent about seeking her out when he had the chance. When the fire was gone, he resolved as he charged forward, he would make everything right between them.

When he reached the old training grounds, he was glad to note that the long grassy strip was not on fire, and the hill at one end of the area was a decent vantage point of the surroundings. He could not stand there for long, however; the wind was blowing the smoke toward him, and he couldn't concentrate well on where it was coming from. After a moment of indecision, he unfurled his wings and prepared to fly toward the hill for a better look.

Bad idea, Idenno warned. *If you fly into that smoke cloud, you'll lose consciousness and fall to your death. We'll have to make our own way to the fire.*

You mean demolish the trees? Deldenno asked with a shudder. The very suggestion of destroying some of the forest horrified him.

We have no choice! If we don't, the trees will be consumed by fire anyway!

Deldenno prepared to argue until something moving in the forest caught his eye. It was human-sized and mostly green. It seemed to be moving toward them, but it moved too erratically for him to get a good look at it. *What is that?*

Idenno squinted. *I do not know, but we should wait to knock down the trees until it is no longer in our way.*

Both Onizards watched carefully until the mysterious something moved onto the forest path and started looking around in confusion. She was human girl with tangled blonde hair, and judging by the simplicity of her green dress and her relative lack of height, she couldn't have been more than nine years of age. When she spun around and saw the two Onizards, her jaw dropped for a few seconds before she began screaming at the top of her lungs.

"No! Not more of them! Mommy! Daddy! Help me!" she shouted when she was coherent. There were many other things she shouted that Deldenno could not understand amongst the loud and shrill screaming. Delden assumed she was either speaking gibberish or something her mommy and daddy would yell at her for later.

Follow the path away from them, Idenno said calmly.

The girl paused her screaming for a moment, blinked a few times and then promptly obeyed, once again screaming for her mommy and daddy.

Why did you do that?

The poor girl has lived out in the wild, and clearly hasn't seen Onizards before. She probably thinks that my mental voice was the Great Lord of the Sky speaking to her or something. She'll be safe once she reaches the Sandleyr. Of course, she'll still be scared of Erfasfi, but then again, everyone is, Idenno sighed. *This is bad, Delden. Her camp must be what is on fire.*

What did she mean, more of them?

Idenno shuddered, and Deldenno could tell he had an idea but wasn't planning on saying anything. *We'll find out once we rescue as many humans as we can. Come, let's put out the fire.*

The elder Child of Water began running through the forest, knocking down any trees that happened to be in front of him. Deldenno followed his lead, being careful to follow Iden's makeshift path whenever possible. After a minute, he found himself in a scene of utter chaos. The remains of several small structures were burning, and a few living human beings were running through the smoke blindly. Some of them were attempting to put out fires that had started on their clothing, while others were screaming names.

"Delma! Run away from here! The dragon won't show any mercy!" one severely burnt man shouted before he collapsed on the ground.

Delden, take care of those buildings, and make sure any healthy humans find the path to the Sandleyr! Idenno ordered before running toward one of the larger buildings and using his water breath to douse the flames.

Deldenno stared in shock at the man on the ground. *Sir, are you okay? Let me help you.*

"Dear Lord, take care of Delma…take care of her," the man said, his voice barely above a whisper.

Sir, who is Delma? the Onizard asked, desperate to discover the meaning behind the man's request.

The man said no more.

Deldenno turned away in frustration and sadness. Whoever or whatever Delma was, he would have to find her and take care of her. Deldenno was not the Onizard to deny the request of a dying person.

When he doused the last of the houses, he noticed a group of humans huddled together, staring toward him in terror. *Don't be frightened; you're safe now. Everything's fine.*

A blast of fire came from behind him, completely charring his wings and killing the last of the humans. Deldenno fell to the ground in pain, then began trembling when he saw the source of the blast.

Her skin was dark orange and scarred in many places, and, though her body was muscular, she was almost as thin as Idenno. She had the appearance of an Onizard who had seen many battles and become stronger and more deadly as a result. Her crimson eyes glimmered with an intense glare of hatred. But the most frightening thing about her was the hideous gash underneath her left eye. Only one Onizard bore that scar, and she had earned it by murdering many Onizards and humans.

Deybralfi, Idenno said as he stepped closer to Deldenno, his mental voice seemingly filled with a mixture of fear and anger.

The Leyrque Rulsaesan and Lady Teltresan certainly sent an interesting pair, she said, calmly walking over to Deldenno and examining his wings. *Deldenno, Bond of my ex-son, and Idenno the pathetic Watchzard. A very odd choice indeed.*

I am no longer Watchzard, Idenno said. Deldenno could tell that he was trying to hide his fear.

A pity; you were always the more observant one. The Sandleyr would have been better off if you had stayed its Watchzard. As it is, since mighty Senraeno did not arrive to control this fire, I shall have to take a hostage to lure him into a confrontation with me.

Deybralfi gripped Deldenno's back leg, broke it with eerie calculation, and lifted him onto her back as he screamed from the shockwaves of pain.

Don't you dare, Deybralfi! Idenno shouted.

You have no hold over me, Idenno. I will not have you spoil my revenge, she said as she took off, carrying Deldenno over the forest.

Deldenno winced in pain as he watched Idenno following him, and he cursed himself for not observing the ex-Fire Queen sooner. He knew that he was going to die regretting his moment of weakness.

Chapter 3

Xoltorble frowned and paced around the Watchzard rock. It wasn't fair that he was always being treated like an immature hatchling. While it was true that his brother was not an adult by any means, Xolt knew that there was a major difference between them. Erfasfi was unBonded, and Xolt was Bonded. When the two of them hatched, Erfasfi had chosen to keep his mind unlinked to anyone else. Xolt, however, had become telepathically linked to another, and he would carry that burden for the rest of his life. When his Bond felt pain, Xolt would feel pain. When his Bond died, he would die as well. Very few Onizards Bonded, but those who did were usually more mature than their unBonded siblings, for they learned many things from the mind of their Bond. Xolt felt lucky that he had chosen someone so intelligent to be his Bond.

"Xoltorble! Why did you leave me behind!" shouted a young man with brown hair and blue eyes. A Child of Water was carrying him out of the entrance, and they both appeared exhausted.

Xolt sighed. *Bryn, you were taking care of your precious Jena, and I knew you were going to take forever! Honestly, I hope you don't give me whatever she's got. The way she can't keep down her food is scary. How can you stand it, Senraeno?*

She's not going to give you what she's got, the Child of Water said. *I haven't caught it, so I assume it must be some human disease. You ought to be worried about your Bond.*

"Yeah, Xolt," said Bryn. "You ought to be worried that I'm going to smack you for leaving me behind!"

Sorry Bryn! I swear to the stars, I thought you wanted to stay with Jena. You're usually quite keen to stay with her for long periods of time.

Erfasfi began snickering.

"Thanks, Xolt! Now your brother is going to be commenting on my relationship with my wife for the rest of the day."

Sorry! Xoltorble said as he winced. This was turning out to be a bad day indeed.

Such immaturity; no wonder Idenno wanted me to keep an eye on you, said the Child of Earth as she rolled her eyes.

Senraeno looked at her and blinked a few times. *Ransenna, what are you doing here?*

I wanted to just get a nice breath of fresh air, but then Idenno and Deldenno put these two under my care to go investigate that smoke cloud, Ransenna said. *I agreed, because I thought they'd be more mature than rumor says they are. But I should have known better; they are young boys, after all.*

What smoke cloud?

Xolt turned and looked toward where the smoke cloud had been. There were a few grey clouds around the general area, but the black smoke cloud was completely gone.

Oh, she said. *They must have put out the fire. I'm sure they'll be back soon.*

Xolt was not so certain; from the way the Child of Earth was pacing about nervously all of a sudden to the way Bryn had started frowning, everyone but Erfasfi seemed to be utterly worried. The young Child of Wind had to wonder why they were so worried; it was rather unusual to have a wildfire at that time of the year, but surely two Children of Water could have handled it?

A series of loud and high-pitched screams echoed across the area, startling everyone. Xolt nearly crashed into Senraeno from jumping back; Ransenna actually did stumble over the Watchzard rock before she stood up in an overly dignified manner.

Was that Uncle Mek? Erfasfi asked as he trembled.

No, stupid, he's only able to stay awake at night, said Xolt.

Bryn squinted in the direction of the scream, and then he began to laugh. "It's okay, little girl, you don't have to be afraid of us."

A human girl peeked from behind a tree near the entrance to the path. She had light blonde hair with several random leaves stuck in it. Said hair looked like it hadn't been combed in months. Her green dress was slightly better off than her hair, though it was somewhat tattered, as if it had gotten caught on something in the woods. Her blue eyes were widening more each second she stared at the Onizards. "Run away, mister! They'll eat you!"

The Onizards all laughed at the suggestion.

I think he'd taste rather terrible, said Erfasfi.

Jena would kill me, said Senraeno.

I would kill me, Xolt said.

Who could have given you such a terrible idea? Ransenna asked.

The girl held her hands to her head and cringed. "Where are all of these voices coming from? Am I going crazy? Please tell me this is a dream."

Bryn stepped toward her. "The Onizards are speaking to you. They speak directly to your head instead of talking out loud like we do."

"You mean the dragons can talk?"

Yes, we can, said Senraeno. *But we are not dragons, we are Onizards.*

What's a dragon? Erfasfi asked.

I think it's a demon Onizard, said Xoltorble. *She's screaming like it is one, anyway.*

"Ignore the fools over there. My name is Bryn. I'm sure we can give you some hospitality until we can figure out where your parents are."

The girl frowned. "My name is Delma. I know where my parents are; they're back where our camp is. Or was; the dark orange dragon set it on fire, and then I ran all the way here. One of the two blue Owneezards must have talked to me; I heard someone tell me to run down that path."

Bryn looked down the path as he stepped back and frowned. "We'd better get you inside, Delma. There's no telling if the dragon will come this way."

I'm sure Deldenno and Idenno would have been able to handle any problem they may have faced, Ransenna said softly.

"Nevertheless, Delma has run a long way; I'm sure she'd be glad for some rest inside."

I will take you both in, said Xoltorble.

I'll go with you guys, said Erfasfi.

Jena will probably need me as well, Senraeno chimed in.

I think I'll remain outside for a while, said Ransenna. *After all, I'll finally be able to get a breath of fresh air without the rest of you bothering me.*

"Okay, let's get you inside, Delma."

"Is it safe?" the girl asked, shuddering as if terrified to go into the dark Sandleyr entrance.

"Of course. I'd trust Xolt here with my life."

You don't have any choice in that, Bryn.

"I'd still trust you with my life. Anyway, Delma, it really is safe. You might be nervous the first time flying on Xolt's back, but if you stay here for any length of time you'll get used to it."

"I'm not staying here long, but thanks," Delma said as she slowly stepped toward Xolt.

Xolt cautiously picked up the two humans with his tail and lifted them onto his back. When he was certain they were safe, he unfurled his wings and flew into the Sandleyr entrance.

Chapter 4

Ransenna was panicking, but she hid it until the others had gone inside the entrance. The girl had mentioned a dark orange dragon. She had to assume that she was talking about an Onizard, for dragons were completely mythical creatures. There was only one dark orange Onizard who would destroy a human village. Now, instead of feeling sad that Deldenno had not noticed her, Ransenna felt guilty for sending him into terrible danger.

For that matter, Ransenna felt a bit guilty for crushing on him. There was a ten year age difference between them, but that was to be expected when before he was born there was a time in which no Onizards had any children whatsoever. Besides, the age difference wasn't a real problem; one of Deldenno's sisters, Amsaena, had already become someone's joinmate. The real problem was that they were both Bonds. Ransenna was the Bond of Deldenno's brother, Delculble, and Deldenno was the Bond of Delbralfi, an Onizard who didn't really trust her. While no one would frown on a relationship between Ransenna and Deldenno, things would be awkward between them and their Bonds for a while. That was assuming, of course, that Deldenno ever actually noticed her. So far, that didn't seem likely to happen. They'd shared one dance at Amsaena's joinmating ceremony before he stepped away for "duty", and only a few shy conversations since.

Ransenna snapped out of her musings when she heard another scream. Someone was hurt! Why hadn't Deldenno or Idenno called for her, when her powers of healing were clearly needed?

The Child of Earth noticed two objects fly above the trees in the distance, and narrowed her eyes as she tried to get a better glimpse of them. At first she saw that they were both blue, and thought that Deldenno and Idenno were returning to the Sandleyr unharmed. But on second glance, she noticed that one of the dots in the distance was also orange, and both were moving quickly away from the Sandleyr. Ransenna panicked briefly before she decided to follow them. There would be a need for healing before the day was over.

They flew far away from the safety of the Sandleyr; Ransenna could feel herself tiring out as she flew over the seemingly unchanging and never-ending forest. Then, probably several hours after they started, the two objects finally landed in a large area of burnt land. Ransenna was careful to land gently by the forest edge, where she would blend in with the dark leaves of the untouched trees. Silently, she walked around the edge of the forest while she tried to figure out what exactly was happening.

You cannot win, Idenno; I am Fire Queen.

The last time I checked, Rulsaesan was still Leyrque of the Sandleyr. You rule nothing.

You are wrong. I have controlled this land for six years, wandering as I pleased. I am Queen over everything you see. Meanwhile, you are still nothing but a Watchzard.

Idenno cringed at the mention of the title he once bore, but otherwise he seemed perfectly calm. It surprised Ransenna to see an Onizard apparently unafraid of the wretched demon. *Very well, Fire Queen,* Idenno said. *I accept your authority here. Just give me Deldenno so I can take him home.*

Ransenna gasped; she could see that Deldenno was lying on the ground behind the Fire Queen. His wings were badly burned, and his leg was broken. No wonder the Fire Queen had to carry him all this way; he was in very poor condition. In fact, if he wasn't healed soon, he would never return to the Sandleyr. Ransenna wished she could think of a way to rescue him on her own, but she knew that the Fire Queen's flames would hit her before she even had a chance to get any closer. Idenno would have to rescue him.

Please, you'll never get back, said the Fire Queen. *I can see you're already tired from the long journey here. If you try to fight me, you'll hurt yourself more than me.*

So be it, Idenno said, his mental voice perfectly monotone.

Uncle Iden, get out of here! Get help! Deldenno screamed.

You ought to listen to your namesake; you're making a fool out of yourself.

I would only be a fool if I left him behind. I made a promise to Rulsaesan, and I intend to keep it. I will not let harm come to Delden, not while I can still fight.

That is your problem, the Fire Queen said. Before Idenno had time to react, she flew beside him and knocked him down. *You can't fight. You never could. Now you will pay for getting in the way,* she said as she carved a deep gash in his chest with her claws.

Ransenna screamed in horror, unable to control her voice. When she realized her error, she froze in place, as if this would somehow help.

Who was that? the Fire Queen asked, looking in Ransenna's direction. Her eyes narrowed for a moment before she smirked. *Ransenna, the great Child of Earth turned pathetic Bond. That was very foolish of you to follow me. What did you think would come of it?*

You aren't going to have any hostages if you keep them in that state. You need my healing powers, Ransenna said, attempting to sound calm in her desperation.

Fine, I'll kill you after you heal them. You still lose.

Run and get help! Deldenno shouted.

She'll catch me, and kill me, Ransenna said as she avoided staring at his tear-filled eyes. *I am no fighter,* she admitted as she turned to the Fire Queen. *But if I heal them completely, they will be strong fighters. You caught Idenno off-guard; next time, it will be you who is caught off-guard.*

You are not convincing me to let you live, the Fire Queen said as she scratched the ground with her right front claws, which were still bloody from wounding Idenno.

You can have me heal them enough each day to keep them from dying, but no more than that. I will even help you carry them to a safer location, Ransenna prayed she was guessing the demon's plan correctly. *Just don't let your hostages die before you can get your revenge on Senraeno.*

The Fire Queen paused for a moment, as if considering the merit of this idea. *I warn you, if you*

25

attempt to escape, both you and they will die. I put their deaths solely on you.

I will not run away from you, Ransenna said. She smiled to imply she was not afraid, even though she was utterly terrified. She would never run. She was a Child of Earth, and it was her duty to heal those in need. Like Iden, she could not leave Deldenno behind.

Chapter 5

Delma shivered as the Owneezard entered what was apparently the entrance to his home. It was colder inside than it was outside, and it was much larger as well. There were many ledges by archways leading away from the main area they were in now, and some of them were occupied by more of the Owneezards. They were bowing to the small group she was with for some strange reason. Delma would have been scared if the man her brother's age wasn't there. Bryn seemed nice enough, for a human who lived with dragons who weren't dragons.

"So you've lived here with the Owneezards your whole life?" Delma asked Bryn.

"Since I was about a year or two younger than you," Bryn explained. "That is, if you're nine."

"I'm ten," Delma said, unable to hide her anger. Everyone always got her age wrong!

"Ten years old? Wow, I'm sorry, I had no idea you were so mature."

"Well, I can take care of myself, if that's what that means."

"So you can," Bryn began to laugh. "Well, I've lived here since I was seven. At first, it was against my will; my entire village was kidnapped and brought here to be used as slave labor. At the time, this place, the Sandleyr, was ruled by a very evil Onizard who called herself the Fire Queen. But six years ago, something changed; Jena Bonded Senraeno."

"What does that mean?"

It means my mind is permanently connected to hers, an Onizard explained. From the way everyone looked toward the blue Owneezard, Delma assumed he was Senraeno.

"The Fire Queen justified enslaving humans by saying we were mentally weaker than the Onizards, which meant we couldn't Bond."

"So, when she Bonded, the Fire Queen went away?"

"It's much more complicated than that, but yes. Jena and Senraeno eventually helped end the reign of the Fire Queen. Then peacetime came, people started marrying right and left-"

Or becoming joinmates. There have been plenty of new Onizard couples as well, Senraeno said.

Yeah, that's kinda important, the dark grey Onizard who was carrying her said. Xolt was his name, wasn't it?

"Fine, Onizards started joinmating right and left, and I ended up Bonding Xolt here."

You ended up marrying Jena as well. One would hope you'd consider that rather important, Senraeno said.

"It is important! I mean, it's my highest priority! I mean…"

He doesn't know what he means, Xolt said.

The pale orange Onizard began to snicker.

"I wouldn't laugh if I were you, Erfasfi. Your dad is the one who blurted out his love for your mom in front of the whole Sandleyr while she was unconscious."

You're the one who nearly got himself killed shouting sentimental nonsense about Jena being the brightest star in the heavens, Erfasfi said. *At least my dad thought he was telling my mom directly.*

"That's different. I thought I was going to be reunited with her in death. How did you find out about that?"

Rulsaesan told me about how she had to rescue you. That must've been embarrassing, Erfasfi said. *I still laugh whenever I think of a Child of Light rescuing mighty Zarder Bryn.*

Delma blinked a few times. "You guys are all weird."

You're very smart and observant, Senraeno said.

"No one in my village has ever argued like that."

They probably don't want you to hear it, because they think you're too young, Xolt said as he landed. *People hide things from Erfasfi and me all the time. It's not fair! I'm nearly two years old!*

"Two?" Delma started to giggle. "That means I'm older than you! You're just a baby."

I am not a baby! Xolt shouted, causing several nearby Onizards to stop and stare in his direction. After a few nearby female Onizards started snickering, Xolt turned slightly red as he lifted Delma and Bryn off his back and onto the ground.

"Onizards age faster than humans," Bryn said quickly. "Xolt is an adult now, and has been since his first birthday."

"That's not fair!"

I know! I wish people would start treating me like an adult!

"You have to start acting like one first," said the voice of a human female.

Delma blinked and turned to see a woman stepping out of one of the nearby archways. She was slightly pale, and seemed tired, but she still walked as if she had pride and purpose. She was wearing a simple pair of grey pants and a shirt that looked like it had been worn for years. Her dark red hair was held back with a scrap of grey fabric, and her brown eyes glimmered as she glanced in Bryn's direction.

"Jena, you're feeling better!" Bryn said happily, walking over to her and hugging her.

"I am. I don't know how long that will last, though. Teltresan said I wasn't contagious, though, so you don't need to worry about catching anything from me. She seemed to find that question rather amusing; she can hardly control her laughter."

Are you sure you can trust my mom? Xolt asked.

"She was a Child of Earth once, you know."

Not for long, said a female Onizard. *But I can still tell you that she isn't contagious.*

Delma stared in awe as this Onizard appeared behind Jena. She was nothing like the other Onizards Delma had seen before; her saffron skin shined almost as brightly as the strange orb at the end of her tail. She held her wings at her side, making herself appear smaller than she actually was, but that did not matter, for every other creature nearby bowed to her. Delma followed suit, figuring she was some important chieftain.

I thought we agreed that we wouldn't have these silly formalities, she said. *If Leyrque Rulsaesan doesn't want you to bow to her, you shouldn't bow to me.*

"My apologies, Lady Teltresan," Bryn said. "How do you know Jena isn't contagious?"

Well, I would assume she must know-where did this little girl come from? Teltresan said as she turned her light green eyes toward Delma.

She was screaming about dragons burning her village, Erfasfi explained.

"I asked Xolt to bring her inside. I thought it best," Bryn said.

"Why didn't you introduce her sooner, Bryn? She must be scared, being separated from her family," Jena said as she turned toward Delma as well. "What is your name?"

"Delma, ma'am."

"Delma? That is a very nice name. It's very close to my mother's name."

"Thank you, ma'am. Your name is nice, too."

What is this about dragons? Teltresan asked. She was frowning, as if she had been given unexpected and frightening news.

"My people have been roaming the woods for some time, trying to find a new home. We had been attacked before, but most of us escape each time," Delma explained as she fought back tears. "This time, I was playing in the woods when I saw it come again. This time, our scouts weren't expecting it, and the dark orange dragon started burning down the houses we were building."

How did you manage to escape this dragon? Teltresan asked.

"I did what any smart person would have done; I ran away."

The Onizards all smiled and nodded.

"We need to send as many able-bodied Onizards out there as possible," Jena said. "Senraeno and I can lead one search party, and Iden can-"

Iden and Delden are out there still, Xolt said.

"What?" Jena exclaimed. "We definitely need a search party, then! Senraeno, let's go!"

Jena, that would not be a good idea, Teltresan said.

"Your joinmate's Bond is out there! We can't leave him to suffer!"

No, we cannot, said yet another voice. *But we can't rush without planning things first.*

Delma groaned. How many of these weird people were there? She turned around and saw another Onizard much like the one called Teltresan. She had golden skin, but she was taller, and she seemed older somehow. She definitely noticed Delma more quickly than Teltresan had; her grey eyes turned to Delma almost immediately.

Good day, young one. I am Leyrque Rulsaesan. Don't worry, you'll get used to the weirdness soon enough.

"How did you…?"

Know you thought I was weird? Teltresan and I have powers of ultimate empathy; we can sense the emotions of those around us. I assumed you thought I was weird because I could sense your confusion.

We couldn't get away with anything when we were younger, Erfasfi said, a note of sadness in his voice. *Mom always could tell when we were feeling guilty.*

Which was almost a constant state with those two, Teltresan said.

"This is all weird," Delma sighed, sitting down on the ground and holding her hands to her head.

And it's only going to get weirder. Teltresan, I was just coming to tell you that Delbralfi is ill.

Teltresan turned pale. *My Delbralfi? No…how can I help him?*

What? Dad! This is all Jena's fault! He caught what she had! Xolt shouted in obvious distress.

It is not like that, Xoltorble; he is ill because Deldenno is hurt. The Fire Queen is speaking through him to Delbralfi, and the news is grim.

What does she want? asked Senraeno. Suddenly, his words seemed full of venom.

You, Rulsaesan said as she closed her eyes and bowed her head. *She says that if the Zarder and human-Bond do not come to confront her within a week, all three of her hostages will die, and their blood will be on us.*

Three hostages? Who is the other hostage? Xolt asked. *Don't tell me Ransenna went after them.*

She did. But we should be glad of that, for apparently Idenno and Deldenno are both gravely injured. If she does not continue to heal them, they will die.

From her vantage point on the ground, Delma could see that Rulsaesan was trying to keep from crying.

"We have no choice, then," Jena said. "Senraeno and I must go."

No, said Rulsaesan. *You are not going anywhere in your condition.*

She isn't that sick, and Teltresan said she wasn't contagious! Senraeno shouted.

"As much as I don't want to see Jena get hurt, Senraeno's right," Bryn said. "You have no good reason to keep her behind. Jena has proven herself consistently to be the strongest Zarder, and Senraeno is the only Onizard to defeat the Fire Queen in battle."

"Actually, you're wrong. Lady Delsenni has as well," Jena said.

And I helped Senraeno, Teltresan said, sounding rather annoyed at Bryn for forgetting this. *I nearly got myself killed to help him defeat the Fire Queen.*

"Nevertheless, Jena and Senraeno are the logical choice. We can't let the Fire Queen just kill five people."

No, we cannot, said Teltresan. *But we can't let her kill eight people, either.*

"Your math is messed up, Teltresan; there are only seven people at risk if you count Jena, Senraeno, the hostages, and the Bonds of those captured," Bryn said.

No, it isn't, Rulsaesan said. *She's counting everyone at risk.*

"How is that possible?" Jena asked.

Well, perhaps you should ask your husband if you don't know. He is technically at fault, Teltresan said, grinning as she stared at the ground.

Partially at fault, you mean, Rulsaesan said. *He and Jena are both at fault here.*

Bryn's jaw dropped and his eyes widened. "You mean...Jena's...wow!"

"I'm...? Really? Seriously?" Jena stammered, holding Bryn's hand and grinning like she had no cares in the world.

"What's going on?" Delma asked. She couldn't believe it, but now things were even more confusing.

Jena's going to have a baby, Xolt said.

Erfasfi snickered. *And we were all worried about catching what she had.*

Well, only the females here have to worry about that, Rulsaesan said.

"Not from me!" Bryn exclaimed.

"And Delma certainly doesn't have to worry about that for some time," Jena added.

Delma just smiled and nodded. She was beginning to think confusion was a normal state in this place.

"This still leaves the matter of who is going to rescue the three hostages," Jena said as a frown began to form on her face. "I don't want any of them to die because I can't rescue them."

"What is a Zarder?" Delma asked.

A Zarder is a human who is Bonded to an Onizard, Senraeno said. *It's a word I made up when I was little.*

"You were little?"

Yes, he was, Rulsaesan said. *He was small enough for Jena to carry him. Now my babies have grown up and are getting more death threats. I had thought I could protect them for just a while longer,* she added as tears ran down her cheek.

Mom, it's okay; we'll figure something out, and we'll rescue Delden and Iden, Senraeno said.

"Why does everyone say Jena is the one she wants?" Delma asked, "There's at least two Zarders in the Sandleyr."

"There are only two." Bryn said. "But the Fire Queen only knows about one of us. Still, Xolt and I are fully capable of going in Jena's place."

The Fire Queen's wrath will be great when she learns it is not Jena coming to the rescue of the hostages, Teltresan said.

"Well, her wrath is generally great anyway. I'd rather have me be the one to inspire it than risk Jena and our child."

I can do this, Mom, Xolt said. *You and Dad have taught me many things, and now I can use your advice to help the hostages.*

Xoltorble, if you fail-

If I fail, Dad will die. I'm not going to let that happen.

"I won't let that happen either," Bryn said. "As much as we tease each other, Bral is my friend. He risked his life for me once; I owe him that favor now."

We have no choice, Rulsaesan said. *Bryn, you and Xoltorble will have to find the Fire Queen and challenge her, but only long enough to allow Ransenna to heal the hostages. Then all of you can flee.*

"I can help you find her!" Delma said. "If she's the orange dragon, I mean. I saw where she came from."

I'm not sure that's the best idea, Delma, Rulsaesan said.

"You can't keep me trapped here! I need to find my family, too!"

Rulsaesan and Teltresan looked at each other for a few moments before Teltresan said, *No, we cannot keep you here. But we hope that if you don't find your family, you will run as soon as you see any sign of trouble.*

"Running is what I'm best at!" Delma said proudly. "But I'll find my family. I know it."

If she's going, I will go, said yet another Onizard as he stepped into the group. He was grey like Xoltorble, but darker, and his eyes were the same color as Rulsaesan's eyes. *Ransenna is my Bond, and I owe my life to Jena.*

"No you don't," Jena said. "That was just instinct. Anyone else would have swum after you as well."

Delculble, I need you here, Rulsaesan said, cutting off an explanation for that strange comment. *You can find out what's going on from Ransenna without stressing your brother and Delbralfi further. Besides, you don't like watching Ransenna work if there's blood. You have a heart that will be crushed if you face that demon who has your brother.*

"How many children do you have?" Delma asked Rulsaesan after she did the math.

Five, Delculble said. *I'm the one with heart, apparently.*

That is a good thing, Rulsaesan said. *Don't let anyone tell you otherwise.*

"Delculble, I will not let her harm Ransenna," Bryn said. "If it is debt to Jena that you feel, please protect her and my child while I'm gone."

Delculble seemed to stand several feet taller. *I will be her most loyal guard after Senraeno.*

Then it is settled. Rulsaesan said before she turned to Xoltorble, Bryn, and Delma. *All three of you should get a good night's rest before leaving tomorrow.*

"I will talk to Lady Delsenni about the news, both good and bad," Jena said.

"Xolt and I will also talk to Leyrkan Mekanni for some advice," Bryn said. "I'm sure we can always use more of his help."

Chapter 6

Bryn and Jena stood by the Watchzard rock, waiting for the Leyrkan and Lady of Night. It was a warm night, unlike some of the nights before it; there was no mist hiding the forest or the Leyr Grounds from view, and there were no clouds obscuring their view of the stars. Overall, if the news he had to give Mekanni and Delsenni was not so grim, Bryn would have thought it was a perfect night, for at the moment it was just him, his wife, and the stars.

Bryn had always found comfort in the stars, even before he knew of the Onizard belief that the stars were the spirits of the dead. Sometimes he thought he could imagine exactly which star was the spirit of his lost family or Jena's mother, but he didn't like to dwell on it. The mystery of the stars was vital to Bryn; if he didn't know who was who, each star was important, and each death had its own significance that was lost when he started trying to pick out people he knew.

"It's a beautiful night," Jena said. "I hope Mek doesn't get sick when we tell him the news."

"Why would Mek get sick? He hasn't been sick in months."

"Bad news about the Fire Queen usually triggers it, and when he finds out his son is ill because she's kidnapped Delden, there's no telling what could happen."

"You never did explain how exactly that works."

"How what works?"

"How Bral is Mek and Senni's son. I don't understand how that could be true."

Jena started blushing. "Well, when two Onizards love each other very much, I'd assume it is the same as with humans," she said with a teasing glance.

"That's not what I meant," Bryn said quickly. He grinned because he knew he was turning crimson now. "How did Bral end up thinking he was the Fire Queen's son for all of those years? It doesn't make any sense to me."

"It didn't to me either. At least, not until I saw Mek and Senni's memories," Jena said as she shuddered. "That is not something you need to see. Some memories should be buried."

"Yes, they should," Bryn agreed to allow for a change of subject. "But some memories should be treasured. I will always treasure the memory I have of when I found out that you were still alive."

Jena smiled. "And I will always treasure the memory of when I found out you weren't entirely crazy for screaming that I was the brightest star in the heavens."

Bryn laughed and wrapped his arm around her. "I hope to share many more treasured memories with you and our child."

Jena nodded and sighed, and both Zarders stopped speaking for a while. Bryn could tell that Jena was just as nervous about the upcoming mission as he was. While he did not doubt Xolt's abilities, he did not know if Xolt was capable of confronting an

Onizard like the Fire Queen. Xolt was a strong adult now, but he had grown up in a Sandleyr where the Fire Queen was nothing more than a figure of stories told to frighten young Onizards. He had never experienced the feeling of helplessness that came when it seemed death was imminent and cold red eyes watched your fear in delight. Bryn was scared, for who could know how Xolt would react if their mission was not a complete success? Who could possibly believe that success was even possible when the Fire Queen had already defeated two of the most powerful Children of Water?

"Mek and Senni should be here soon," Jena said as she leaned on Bryn's shoulder.

Bryn smiled. Jena always knew how to make him feel stronger than he really was. "They'll probably wait," Bryn said. "They've more than likely been told about all of the news already, and if I know Lady Delsenni she's encouraging everyone to give us some alone time to be lovebirds."

"Senrae promised not to tell! If they've found out, it's Xolt's fault."

What's my fault? the Child of Wind asked as he flew out of the entrance. *I didn't do anything except help that little human girl go to sleep and tell Grandpa Mek and Grandma Senni to come up here.*

Happy news? asked Mekanni, Leyrkan of Night, as he followed Xolt. Bryn instinctively avoided looking at Mekanni's legs. The first time he had met Mekanni, he had stared too long at the black Onizard's completely mangled left legs, and the Leyrkan had gotten sick. Mekanni's version of sick meant much screaming and rambling about eyes trying to get him before invariably his mate Lady Delsenni calmed him down. She had to listen to him call her Senfi for a while, but her voice calmed him.

That did not lessen Bryn's fear of making Mekanni sick, for what the Leyrkan did before Delsenni calmed him down was completely unpredictable.

Do tell us, Delsenni said as she followed closely behind Mekanni. Like Mekanni, she was black like the sky without stars, the complete opposite of Rulsaesan and Teltresan of the Day Kingdom. Unlike Mekanni, part of her front horn was broken off, and her golden eyes contrasted sharply to Mekanni's lavender eyes. The two curved horns on her head stood out more than the curved horns did on most Onizards, but that was because their saffron hue contrasted sharply against the rest of her body. Her horns and eyes glistened in the light from the orb on Mekanni's tail.

"Lady Delsenni and Leyrkan Mekanni, I should probably tell the worst news first," Jena said. "Deldenno, Idenno, and Ransenna have all been kidnapped."

What? How is this possible? Delsenni asked, glancing quickly in Mekanni's direction.

The eyes...they got them. Iden, I tried to warn you. I tried to protect you by telling you to protect Rulsaesan. Don't let them get anyone else! Mekanni exclaimed, shuddering as he stared off at unseen things.

"We won't, Leyrkan. You're safe from the eyes. Senfi will protect you," Jena said slowly.

Mekanni froze, shook his head a few times, then sighed. *Thank you, Jena. This is terrifying news. Why did she kidnap them? Normally she just kills.*

"She's holding them as hostages in an attempt to lure Senraeno and me there."

Oh Jena, I'm so sorry, Delsenni said as she bit her lip.

"I'm not letting her go. I'm taking her place," Bryn said.

Bryn, wanting to aid your mate is an honorable thing, but you must be careful, Mekanni said. *I'm not sure you and Xolt can handle that responsibility or the pain if something goes wrong.*

"We have no choice. Jena and I have a different responsibility now."

Don't tell me you've decided that you've suddenly decided to choose the traditional roles for men and women from ancient human culture, Delsenni said. *Jena is stronger than you in many ways, Bryn; she ought to be the one who goes to rescue them.*

"That is what he said too," Jena said. "Until we learned that I am pregnant."

Pregnant? Delsenni asked, her eyes widening almost as much as her grin. *That is a different matter entirely. By all means, don't go fighting the Fire Queen when you have an unborn child to protect, especially when you and Bryn have been waiting so long for a child.*

I'm sure they enjoyed waiting, though, Mekanni said as he smirked at Bryn.

Bryn hid his face with his hands for a moment before realizing it was all in vain; the two Children of Light could sense clearly that he was embarrassed, and Xolt could tell through their mind link. He wasn't going to be fooling anyone. It comforted him, though, that Jena was blushing just as much as he was.

Mekanni! Delsenni shrieked as she gave him a glare and held up her tail as if she was threatening to hit him.

What? None of us are children here, other than Jena's child, who cannot hear us.

Still, I'd rather have not heard that, Xolt said. *Especially coming from my grandpa.*

Fine. To please you all, I will say no more other than to congratulate Jena and Bryn. Mekanni shrugged and smiled. *Have you two picked out a name yet?*

"We just found out today. We haven't had time to really plan anything yet," Jena said.

Well, by all means take your time. You'll know when you find the right name, Mekanni said.

Bryn, I'd suggest that you get some rest now, Delsenni said. *I assume you will be starting your journey tomorrow.*

"I will. I hope to make this a safer world for my son or daughter."

A safer world for our children; it is all anyone can hope for, Mekanni said. *I only hope that is not an impossible ideal.*

Chapter 7

Ransenna focused her eyes on the stars and tried not to cry as she listened to the screaming.

Deldenno was safe, or at least not being injured further; the Fire Queen had for the most part ignored him. After all, he was not going to die any time soon, and he could not fly away either. Ransenna had tried to convince the Fire Queen to let him go free; what need had she for three hostages, when two would suffice? But she would not listen, and she threatened Ransenna before Idenno distracted her with threats of his own. The Fire Queen then ordered Ransenna to give more healing to Idenno before she carried him off to a more secluded area. Since that time, she had heard nothing but the screaming and the sound of Delden's frantic hyperventilation out of fear.

This reminded Ransenna too much of the life she lived before she knew the true nature of the Fire Queen. It was a dark time in her life, when she felt that no one could possibly love her, and so she inflicted hatred on the world. The Fire Queen had liked her then, when she could not see that human beings had souls as valuable as Onizard souls. It was the time when she was forced to ignore the screams at night, the screams that echoed in her heart still.

We're going to die out here, Deldenno said as he started shuddering. *We're all going to die, one by one!*

We will be fine, Ransenna said in an attempt to reassure him. *We will all get out of this alive after Senraeno rescues us.*

She's hurting him, Delden said as he started to cry. *She's hurting him, and he could have just stayed behind and waited for Senraeno to come instead of throwing himself in the middle of this. All of this is my fault.*

Don't say that! Ransenna said firmly. *If we start throwing a pity party for ourselves, we'll never get out of this alive. Never feel guilt over someone loving you enough to protect you. You should only feel guilt if you start believing that no one in this world loves you.*

Deldenno took a few quick, deep breaths. *Thank you…what was your name again?*

You're welcome, Deldenno. I am Ransenna.

You should have run away when you had the chance, Ransenna.

And let the both of you die? I could not live with that guilt.

Do you really think we're going to live through this just by you being here?

Ransenna smiled in spite of what she was really feeling. *Of course we are. Idenno is probably just screaming to hide that he's gathering his strength. Then, when Senraeno comes, they will both defeat the Fire Queen once and for all!*

I hope so, Delden said. *I'd hate to see someone beautiful like you die on my account.*

And that is how I know you need your rest; you're starting to say delusional things, Ransenna said calmly as she sat down next to him. *Just get some rest, and start to recover your strength.*

Deldenno smiled and closed his eyes, and after a few minutes Ransenna could hear him breathing deeply as he drifted off into sleep. She was glad; in sleep, he was protected from the screams.

Chapter 8

Give up, the Fire Queen said as she slowly stepped away from Idenno. She was panting and acting as if she were exhausted, but smiling from a torture well executed.

Give up what? The Child of Water asked. He desperately hoped that Delden had not heard him screaming; the younger Onizard needed to keep his innocence. Iden didn't want anyone worrying about him or guessing at what had happened. He was deeply ashamed about the assault, but he was not surprised; he had guessed enough from how Mekanni acted after his battle with the Fire Queen. He knew what to expect when the Fire Queen had complete control over a male Onizard. He just had to make certain that Delden did not suffer as he had.

Your sickening desire to protect the others, she said as she glared at him with those frightening eyes of hers. *It is keeping you from caring about yourself. I cannot enjoy myself as much when you're holding back your screams.*

Why would I want you to "enjoy yourself" more, you demon? Iden said, though he did not shout it as loudly as he felt like shouting it. He had no idea how close Delden was, and how much he could hear.

You want to live, do you not? She said, stepping closer and holding her tail flame over his throat.

If it is my time to die, I will die; if it is not, then I have nothing to fear, Idenno said.

No, I forgot; you always put others before yourself, the Fire Queen said, shaking her head and lifting her tail flame away from his throat. *Noble Idenno, heir of Senbralni, must always put others first, especially if they're related to his precious Rulsaesan.*

I am no longer the heir of Senbralni, Idenno said, blinking at the strange title. As far as he was aware, no one had mentioned the heir of Senbralni since Delsenni gained her powers. *Who my ancestors were does not define me.*

You can't drop a title like that, you fool, the Fire Queen said, shaking her head. *You're supposed to be the one starting a big happy family of Senbralni heirs while your brother stands off to the sidelines to be wooed by Onizard women of lesser blood.*

Where had this come from? Idenno thought everyone had forgotten or had ceased to care that he was the older twin. *I know you're seeing the events from a completely skewed angle, but Delsenni has proven herself to be among the greatest heroes of the Onizards. I have no need to produce heirs of my own blood when there are plenty of heirs of Senbralni to choose from. Besides, Mekanni loves her very much.*

Lusts after her, you mean, the Fire Queen said as she scowled. *There is no such thing as love; I have destroyed everything that claims to be love.*

But you have not destroyed love, Idenno said, grinning in spite of his pain. *You cannot destroy love, no matter how much you try.*

I will destroy your so-called love of your precious Rulsaesan, then, just to prove you wrong, the Fire Queen threatened, stepping uncomfortably close to Iden. It seemed as if she was planning on "enjoying herself" again.

Idenno closed his eyes and sighed. *Go ahead and try. Just leave Delden out of it.*

What?

You heard me; do not use Delden for your pleasure the way you plan on using me.

Him? The Fire Queen laughed, but to Iden it sounded like she was trying to hide her utter disgust at the idea. Iden resisted the urge to smile as he listened to the Fire Queen say, *He's too young! Besides, why would I go near the boy, when I can enjoy myself so much more by making you lose your love of Rulsaesan?*

You won't. The very idea is ludicrous.

We shall see, Idenno. In the meantime, if I don't make you forget Rulsaesan right away, I will at least make you scream for mercy.

Why should I scream for something that will not come? Idenno asked as he silently prayed to the Great Lord of the Sky for the strength to endure the pain to come.

Chapter 9

Bryn, Bral wants to speak to you before you leave, Teltresan said.

Bryn blinked a few times before he completely woke up. *Xolt, tell her I need a minute,* he said privately to his Bond. Though he was perfectly willing to talk to his friend, he had no desire to have Teltresan walk in on him when he was only half-dressed. There was something inherently wrong about a female other than Jena seeing him shirtless, even if she was an Onizard female.

After he carefully lifted Jena's arm off of his chest, Bryn walked over to the pile of clean clothes and grabbed the most readily available clean shirt and pants. Upon a closer inspection that involved a failed attempt to put the clothes on, Bryn realized the pants were actually Jena's pants. He wasn't exactly going to fit in those. Granted, Jena wouldn't fit into them either in a few months, but that was a problem he'd have to worry about when he returned. After he dug through the pile and finally found a pair of his own pants, he changed into them and left the leyr.

Bryn, why did you wake me up? Xolt whined once Bryn was in the Invitation Hall. It was clear from the way Xolt was stumbling about that he was not completely awake yet.

Your father wants to speak to you, Teltresan said as she emerged from her own leyr.

From the way she stared at the ground as she walked, Bryn could tell she was worried. Though it was technically impossible for a Child of Light to stay awake during the time he or she was not ruling, she was acting as if she had been up all night.

Is father alright? Xolt asked, sounding as if he sensed the same thing Bryn had sensed.

He's doing well, considering the circumstances, Teltresan said. *He can feel that Deldenno is badly injured. He'd come out here to talk to you, but he's in too much pain to move.*

Is he going to die? Xolt seemed as if he was about to cry.

Certainly not, Teltresan said as she glanced in Bryn's direction. *Apparently Ransenna is healing Delden enough to keep that from happening. But she is no match for the Fire Queen; no one is.*

"You say that because Xolt hasn't fought her yet," Bryn said. "When Xolt goes against her, she will lose again."

I hope you are right, Teltresan said. *Come, let us go see Bral.*

Bryn cautiously stepped toward Delbralfi's leyr, remembering the first time that he had come to that place. He had mistakenly believed Bral was responsible for Jena's untimely death, and he had wanted Bral to suffer greatly for that. It was embarrassing to think about that now, when he was worried about losing one of his best friends to the Fire Queen.

Bryn! the Child of Fire said as the human entered. *And Xoltorble as well. I am glad you both could come. I hope I wasn't interrupting a conspiracy of passion.*

"Jena's still asleep," Bryn said. "Besides, that's no conspiracy. At least I first told her that I loved her when she was conscious."

When she miraculously returned from the dead, after much teasing from Senraeno and me, Bral said. He started to laugh, then winced when his wings moved. *Deldenno has burnt wings and a broken leg,* he explained.

That should be relatively simple for Ransenna to heal, Teltresan said. *Provided, of course, that she can heal him without the Fire Queen burning her alive. It will take much of her time and energy to heal him, especially when she has to deal with Idenno's injuries as well.*

"Xolt and I can distract her for long enough to allow them all to escape."

An excellent idea, Bryn, the Child of Fire said. *You were always good at providing distractions.*

"Not as good as Teltrena was at distracting you. Then she became Teltresan, and she's distracted you even more."

The Child of Fire paused for a moment, looked into the eyes of his joinmate, then said, *Okay, you win. I'm not really in the mood for teasing you.*

"Delden really is sick, then," Bryn said quietly.

I would hope that I'd always distract you, Teltresan said, playfully glaring at him. *After all, you always manage to distract me.*

Can we please stop talking about this? Xolt asked as he stared at the ground. *It's rather embarrassing.*

We'll have to tease him mercilessly when he gets distracted by someone, Bral said.

Indeed, we shall, Teltresan said as she grinned back at him.

"I suppose we'd better get to talking about the mission before Xolt's mind shuts down any more than it already has," Bryn said.

Yes, we must, Bral agreed. *Bryn, take care of the young girl. She's going to go through a rough time when she realizes that her parents are dead.*

Do we know her parents are dead? Xolt asked.

"The Fire Queen never left humans alive when she wanted to kill them," Bryn said slowly.

She won't now, either, Teltresan said. *She'll want to go for the shock value, just to make Rulsaesan and me more likely to send Senraeno after her. She's going to be in a rather bad mood when she finds out that we sent the wrong Zarder.*

"We'll handle it," Bryn said. "I've handled it before."

You won't have the benefit of Rulsaesan's protection out there in the wilderness, Bral warned.

"And the Fire Queen won't have the benefit of my suicidal anger," Bryn said. "It all works out in our favor in the end, especially if Ransenna is able to heal Idenno and Deldenno quickly enough for them to join the fight."

Don't count on the best luck. Count on the worst luck, and hope for the best, Delbralfi said.

"I always do," Bryn said. "Take care of Jena for me while I'm gone, please."

Of course, Delbralfi said. *Just come back to us alive.*

"We will," Bryn said. "Jena will be devastated if we don't. I don't want her shedding tears over my dead body."

I won't keep you any longer, then, Delbralfi said. *Just know you leave with love.*

Chapter 10

Jena awakened to the sound of Bryn pacing about the leyr. He was grabbing random pieces of clothing and throwing them into a sack, mumbling occasionally as he seemed to be searching for some particular item.

Jena resisted the urge to cry as she rose from their bed, hoping he'd stop packing long enough to notice her. If things turned for the worst, she wanted to be able to tell their child that their father left the Sandleyr proud and unafraid, forever Senme like he was only six years ago. But time had changed him, and the boy who didn't care about leaving the world had become a man with responsibilities. He was a man who had found so much to care about in six years, a man who was in love. Six years was such a long time, but it seemed far too short of a time now as the early morning light shone through the Sandleyr entrance.

Bryn turned around, noticed her, and smiled. She could tell he was trying to hide the fear and nervousness he was feeling; she could see that the blue eyes she had grown to love were trying to hold back tears.

Jena tried to laugh, but when she found she couldn't, she resorted to smiling bravely. "Well, I guess it's my turn to think the one I love is dead."

"No it isn't," Bryn said. "I may be vanishing into the unknown, but you won't find my star in the sky for some time."

"I hope so, Bryn," Jena said. "I'm so scared."

"I am too. That doesn't mean we have to give in to that fear."

Jena nodded, then instinctively rested her hand on the necklace she never took off. It was nothing more than a silver chain, but it had belonged to her mother, and having it had always given her strength when all hope seemed to fail. Without another thought, she took it off her neck and placed it in Bryn's hand.

"Why are you doing this?" Bryn asked, his eyes widening as he held the necklace carefully and reverently. He knew the significance of the necklace more than anyone else. Jena knew he watched her holding it when she was feeling sad, for often he'd hold her more tightly when she did so.

"I don't know," Jena admitted. "I guess I just want you to…" she began, before trailing off in thought.

"To what?"

"I-I want you to remember me when times get tough."

Bryn smiled as he carefully placed the necklace back into her outstretched hand. Then he grasped her hand tightly and looked directly into her eyes. "I don't need that to remember you, Jena. You're starting to sound like the patiently waiting lover out of those silly fairy stories our parents told us when we were young. Those weren't real. This is," he said as he pulled her close to him and kissed her passionately. When they parted, he added, "I will return to you. Our child is not going to grow up without a father."

Jena smiled and fought her tears. "You'd better return. Bral would be rather upset with you if you didn't."

"You and Bral and everyone had better welcome back the two newest heroes of the Sandleyr when they return."

"We will," Jena said.

Bryn, Delma is ready. Xolt said as he stepped into the leyr. *Are we leaving now?*

"Yes, we will be in just a moment," Bryn said. Then, he kissed Jena on the forehead one last time before he said, "I love you."

"I love you too, Bryn. Come back alive."

"I will return. I promise," Bryn said as picked up his sack and exited the leyr.

Jena waited until he was completely gone before she began to sob.

Bryn bit his lip as he left the leyr. He knew Jena was hiding the full extent of her emotions from him. It was clear she didn't want him to be as afraid as he was. But he couldn't help it; he had to look at the reality of things. He knew in his heart, though, that he would return. They had already fought too hard to stay alive during the years of the Fire Queen's rule.

"Are you okay, Mister Bryn?" Delma asked as she walked up to the Bonds.

"I'm as okay as a person leaving their home for a while can be. I'm going to miss Jena," he replied.

"Well, once we find my parents, you'll at least be able to relax for a while."

"When we find your parents, Xolt and I are going to have to find our friends."

"I'm sure my village will be happy to give you guys a feast once you've found your friends, though."

Bryn smiled. "I don't think your village will be able to give us a feast. Xolt eats a lot."

I don't eat as much as Erfasfi does! The Child of Wind protested.

In any case, be careful, Delma, Rulsaesan said as she exited her leyr and walked into the Invitation Hall. *If you find the orange dragon again, run away and let Bryn and Xoltorble handle things.*

"You've come to bid us farewell, Leyrque?" Bryn asked as he bowed.

There is no reason for me to bid you farewell. I know you will both return.

Thank you, Leyrque, Xolt said.

"Tell Bral not to worry; he can count on us," Bryn said. "And please make sure Jena is okay. I tried to reassure her, but I think you, Senraeno, and Senni can help her more than I can."

Do not worry, Senme; your wife will be well and awaiting your return.

"Thank you," Bryn said. Then, after he took a deep breath, he said, "Well, Xolt, I think it's time for us to go."

It is, his Bond said as he picked up Bryn and Delma with his tail. Then, when they were situated on his back, he said to Rulsaesan, *Look after my mom and dad. Tell them I'll make them proud.*

You already do, Rulsaesan said softly. Then Xolt took off, and Bryn heard no more.

57

Chapter 11

Wake up, Ransenna, the Fire Queen said gruffly. *We are leaving this place. It is time for you to make yourself useful and prevent the other hostages from dying.*

Ransenna stood up and looked about her surroundings. She had fallen asleep next to Delden; inwardly she cringed, for she knew the Fire Queen was not going to ignore that. He was still sleeping, and she had no desire to wake him up; when he did wake up, his injuries, especially the leg injury, were going to be extremely painful. But she had no choice; carefully, she placed the end of her tail on the leg wound and concentrated on her powers for a moment. Then, just as the wound was starting to heal, the Fire Queen pushed her away.

His injuries are not as critical, the Fire Queen said. *I am no fool; go heal Idenno.*

From the way Iden had been screaming last night, he could have been either badly injured physically or badly injured emotionally. Perhaps even both. Ransenna shuddered and braced herself for what was to come. Slowly she walked over to the area where the Fire Queen had carried off Iden, and saw a sickening sight.

His chest wound was the worst of the injuries; Ransenna was surprised he was even still alive. Then again, rumor had it that Idenno's brother Mekanni had survived greater injuries from the claws of the Fire Queen. The injury by itself was enough to make anyone scream, but from the way Iden was curled up, as if he were back in his egg, Ransenna doubted that was actually why he was screaming. There was something else terribly wrong, and the Child of Earth doubted she wanted to know what that was.

Ransenna carefully placed her tail on the chest wound and began to heal it. Just as it was starting to grow new skin, Idenno woke up and said, *That's enough. I wouldn't want to get you in trouble.*

She hurt you worse than you're willing to admit, Ransenna said as she took her tail away.

I'll live; Idenno started to shrug, but paused as if realizing the stupidity of that particular movement. *Where is Delden? Is he okay?*

Deldenno is fine, other than the wing injury and the broken leg, but I'm helping him with that.

*Good...I promised Rulsaesan...*Idenno said before he started to cringe in pain.

Promised her what, sir? Ransenna asked, trying to get his mind off the injury.

That he'd take her to the stars and show her that they're really made of sweet grass, The Fire Queen said as she stomped past Ransenna and roughly lifted Iden onto her back. *Go do your job and pick up Deldenno.*

Yes, of course, Ransenna said, desperately avoiding the look in Idenno's eyes.

Idenno had the look of an Onizard who had calmly abandoned all hope for the future and was now silently awaiting the end. Ransenna couldn't handle that. She had to have hope that at least one of them would live. If Idenno, the strongest of the three hostages, had already given up hope, there was no hope for her or Deldenno.

Ransenna returned to the place where Deldenno was resting, and gently lifted him onto her back. After she felt him writhe in pain, she said, *I am sorry for this. I hope I am not causing you too much discomfort.*

I'll live. He said. *We must remember to live. Teltresan will kill us if we don't live.*

Ransenna blinked. *I guess you're still delusional.*

No I'm not. It was a joke. A bad joke, but still a joke. We're going to need humor if we want to get out of this alive.

Very well. I think I know a joke, Ransenna said. *Once there was a goose that was pure white, for it had been raised by humans. But it didn't stay where it belonged; it found a family of wild geese and adopted them as its own. Isn't that funny?*

Well, no, Deldenno said. *It didn't really make much sense.*

I guess not. I must be remembering it wrong.

Or maybe it isn't supposed to be a joke at all. It sounds like it's supposed to be one of those stories that is supposed to give an important life lesson.

A life lesson about what?

No one seems to know. But I guess, in a way, it's a story about us.

How so?

Well, I would not call either of us wild geese. But here we are, out in the wild, already calling it our own. We're out of place here.

Ransenna sighed. *I don't think I'll ever call this place home. But let's go; it seems her majesty is ready.*

I am, the Fire Queen said. *You are wasting time, Ransenna. Try my patience again, and both you and Deldenno will fall out of the sky.*

Yes, Fire Queen, Ransenna said calmly, but inwardly she worried. How much had the Fire Queen already guessed about her annoying attraction to Deldenno? She certainly didn't want her feelings to be a burden to everyone involved.

The Fire Queen took off without any further commentary, though she was slow getting into the air due to the weight of Idenno. Ransenna followed, staying a good distance behind in order to avoid conversation with the Fire Queen.

Don't, Deldenno said. Ransenna could not see his eyes, but his voice sounded as if he were calmly pleading for something from her.

Don't what? Ransenna asked. *I'm not hurting you, am I?*

No, I'm fine. Just don't try to escape now. Don't leave Uncle Iden to suffer. I don't want him to die.

I won't, Deldenno. All three of us are going to get out of this alive, Ransenna said. *Idenno was a Watchzard; he'll know when the right time to escape is. In the meantime, we will wait.*

Please try to protect him, Delden pleaded.

I will do my best, but the Fire Queen has been keeping him away from me. She knows he's smart enough and strong enough to get us out of this. Once Senraeno comes, it will all be over for her.

How will Senraeno find us?
He just will. I know it.

After an awkward moment of silence, Deldenno said, *As soon as you get a chance, run away. Run as far as you can while you are still healthy and strong. Don't worry about me. I know you have the Code of Earth telling you that taking care of us is your responsibility, but don't neglect your responsibility to yourself.*

You are rather full of contradictions, Ransenna said. *I will run away only when Senraeno or Idenno tells me to run. Even then, I am not going anywhere if it means letting anyone die. I would never be able to get over the guilt of knowing I was responsible for another's death.*

But it wouldn't be your fault! Deldenno said.

Yes it would, Ransenna said. *I am not going to leave anyone behind, and that's final.*

Deldenno sighed. *I hope Jena finds us soon.*

I hope so too, Deldenno, Ransenna said as she stared at the vast wilderness ahead of her. *I really do hope so.*

Chapter 12

"You're lucky, Mister Bryn," Delma said as they started down the path toward the training grounds. Since they were going slowly to pick up any signs of a trail, all three of the rescuers were walking. Delma rather preferred it that way; even though flying on Xolt's back was convenient, walking seemed much safer.

"Why do you say that?" he asked. "It seems that it's my fate to leave my wife behind while I go off into uncertain danger. I don't like uncertain danger."

He rather prefers certain happiness, Xolt explained as he smirked.

"Then he'll be searching for some time," Delma said.

"That's my luck," Bryn said. "It seems that it's your luck as well, since you're stuck with us."

"I won't be stuck with you for long. I'm going to find my family!" Delma said, as if she were stating a truth delivered from the Great Lord of the Sky.

If you insist, Xolt said. *Now, if we're going to find them, you should probably tell us where the dragon came from and how you got so near to the Sandleyr in the first place.*

"That's a simple story," Delma said. "The dragon came from the north. It was chasing after us."

"Chasing after you?" Bryn asked. "How is that possible?"

If it was chasing after you, you'd be dead by now, Xolt said.

"It was chasing after us!" Delma exclaimed. "It's been coming every so often ever since we left our old village and started out on our own. The village had too many people in it, so my mom and dad said we'd leave. I was only five, so I don't remember much about the old village I just know we've been running from the dragon ever since."

"When did the dragon first appear?"

"I remember my father talking to a strange old man. He said that there was a dragon ahead, but no one believed him, even when he said that the dragon killed his entire village. That night, the dragon first started coming," Delma said. "It's been almost five years now, and the dragon has been coming all the time, always from the north. We thought that we had escaped it; it hadn't shown up for months. But now here I am, with a man and a dragon-like creature, going to find the dragon and my family. I hope we find my family first."

"I hope we find them too," Bryn said.

Bryn, look at this, Xolt said, his tone betraying his worry.

Bryn looked about. At first, he only saw the training grounds and the hill. Then, he noticed a grove of trees that had been completely knocked down, which lead to what Bryn assumed was what was left of the village Delma belonged to.

"Delma, stay here," the Zarder warned.

"Why should I? My family could be there waiting for me to find them!"

That was what Bryn was afraid of, though he could not mention this to Delma. "If your family is there, I will tell you. But in the meantime, Xolt needs someone to keep him company."

No I don't, Xolt protested.

"Yes you do," Bryn said as he glared at his Bond.

"You think I'm going to find them dead, don't you?"

Bryn blinked in surprise. "You're ten years old, and you already know about this stuff?"

"Of course. The dragon has attacked our village before. I'm young, not stupid," Delma said. "If my family is dead, I want to see for myself, and plant a tree for them."

Plant a tree? Xolt asked. *Why, when they went to the stars?*

"Stars? The Lord of the Sky would rather have trees in remembrance of the dead," Delma said. "Don't you plant trees for your dead?"

"We don't," Bryn admitted. "But, if it is your culture to plant trees for the dead, Xolt and I will help you, assuming it comes to that."

But they went to the stars! Xolt complained.

"No, they returned to the earth," Delma said. There was a hint of anger in the young girl's voice.

"Now is not the time to argue," Bryn said. "Come, Xolt, let's go toward the village. Respect Delma's culture, and agree to disagree."

"Maybe they returned to the earth and went to the stars at the same time," Delma said.

Perhaps, Xolt said as he began to walk toward the destroyed village. *Their earthly forms had to go somewhere, so the earth makes sense.*

"According to the people of my village, their spirits return to the earth as well. When we plant a tree for them, their spirits will live on."

"I fear we may be planting many trees today," Bryn said as he looked ahead.

There was nothing of note left to the village. Certainly, there were a few makeshift houses that had only been partially burnt, but those were impossibly waterlogged. Charred and mutilated human bodies were strewn everywhere. Bryn resisted the urge to throw up.

"Mommy! Daddy! Brother!" Delma screamed before she started sobbing hysterically.

That demon will pay for this, Xolt said. *I will kill her myself. Too many have suffered on her account!*

"You would become a murderer like she is to avenge these innocents?" Bryn asked, frowning at his Bond's readiness to kill. It was clear that he didn't understand, and couldn't understand. These people were not close to him; he had not seen those he loved killed by the Fire Queen. "Delma, I am sorry. Do you need help finding tree seeds to plant?"

"Yes, please," Delma said as she half-sobbed, half-sighed. "I guess I'm the last."

"Jena and I are among the last of our village as well," Bryn said.

"What am I supposed to do? Where am I supposed to go? How can I survive without my village, my family, and my friends?"

Bryn sighed and shrugged. "I do not know what future is in store for us. I know that Xolt and I are going to do our best to find the demon who did this to your family and bring her to justice. You can help us if you wish, or you can return to the Sandleyr until you figure out where you are going to go."

"I'd rather help you find the dragon," Delma said. "I don't want her destroying your family too. After that…I don't know. My mommy and daddy were supposed to be smart enough to escape. They should have known better!"

"They couldn't have known what was in store," Bryn said. "I won't pretend that things will be easy, or that they'll slowly get better. Death is a hard thing to face. I do know, though, that you'll always carry the memory of your family with you, and as long as you don't forget them, they will never leave you."

Delma struggled to maintain her composure. Slowly, she looked to Bryn and asked, "Could we look for the tree seeds now, Mister Bryn?"

"Of course," Bryn said. "You probably won't want to talk about it for a while, but if you need to talk to someone about it, I'll listen."

"Thank you," Delma said. "I am glad you and Xolt are my friends. I just hope the dragon isn't hurting your family."

If she is, she will pay for it, Xolt said.

Bryn sighed and looked toward the north. "I hope so."

Chapter 13

Idenno cried out in pain after the Fire Queen casually tossed him to the ground. It was almost impossible for him to breathe with the chest injury, and it didn't help that the Fire Queen had spent most of the journey to this location trying to prove that love didn't exist. She was mad with power, and also a fool. Iden could not be convinced that love didn't exist; he had experienced love almost all of his life.

Her name was originally Rulsaena. She was a Child of Earth more gifted than her peers at healing, for she truly cared about those she healed. She and Deyraeno were Idenno's best friends as he grew up, and when he matured, he began to notice certain things about Rulsaena more. He could see more clearly how beautiful she was. It did not affect his respect of her as his friend; it was his friendship with her that allowed him to see that aspect of her. Over the years, Idenno slowly realized that he loved her.

When his grandfather, Leyrkan Mesenni, found out about Idenno's love, he tried to force Idenno to stay away from her, always mumbling about the heirs of Senbralni being too tied up with the Day Kingdom. Mesenni was always more concerned about Idenno's duty to continue the line of Senbralni. He ignored any faults of Iden's twin brother

Mekanno and blamed Iden for everything that went wrong. He even forbade Deyraeno and Rulsaena from dwelling in the Night Kingdom in an attempt to force Idenno to find a more suitable mate. But this did not stop Idenno from speaking to Rulsaena and Deyraeno; Idenno entirely abandoned the Night Kingdom for the Day Kingdom when he heard this unfair ruling. Somehow, Idenno could always sense his grandfather's disappointment in him, even though it was clear that Mekanno, now Mekanni after their grandfather's death, was the real heir of Senbralni.

Time moved on, and the Leyrque of the Day Kingdom died, naming Rulsaena as her heir. Now that she had become a Child of Light with powers of empathy, Rulsaesan finally realized that Idenno loved her. It was then that she was forced to tell him that she loved Deyraeno. Iden worried that he had hurt her through this knowledge, and hid his own tears to protect her. He swore then that he would always protect her and her family, and their friendship continued to the present day.

Now Iden had no choice but protect Deldenno, son of Rulsaesan and Deyraeno. He would endure the suffering inflicted by the Fire Queen to protect young Delden, just as he had endured the path of the Watchzard to protect Rulsaesan and Deyraeno. He could not live with himself if he did not do everything in his power to protect Deldenno, for he loved Deldenno as if he were his own son. The Fire Queen was more of a fool than he originally suspected if she thought she could prove to him that love did not exist.

Iden had to wonder why she even cared about love's existence in the first place. Of course, love had foiled her plans in the past, but that didn't give her any right to try to prove love did not exist. If anything else, it should have proved to her that love did exist. There was something that Iden didn't understand about this situation, but he was certain that in time the Fire Queen would blurt out that information when he least expected it. For now, he had no choice but to hide his morbid curiousity.

Ransenna, stop paying attention to the whelp and heal the Watchzard, the Fire Queen shouted, temporarily putting an end to Idenno's thoughts.

Idenno watched as the Child of Earth walked toward him. She was trembling in fear as she looked at Idenno's chest wound, but she smiled as she touched it with her tail and gave him enough healing to last for a day longer.

I am sorry about this, sir, Ransenna said. *If I could help you more, I would.*

Deldenno needs you more now, Idenno said calmly. *Don't worry about me.*

Deldenno is not hurt as badly as you are, sir. He does not need me more now.

Yes he does, Idenno said. He now remembered where he had seen her before; Deldenno had been talking about being unable to talk to a beautiful Child of Earth, and as he was speaking she had arrived. He couldn't remember what she needed to say; it was some inane errand Teltresan supposedly sent her on. Idenno didn't believe a word of this, but Deldenno seemed to believe it, which apparently satisfied her.

Enough chatter, Ransenna, the Fire Queen said. *Talk to the whelp if you wish, but you will not speak to Idenno again.*

Yes, of course, Ransenna said as she backed away quickly.

You will address me as Fire Queen if you wish to live.

Yes, Fire Queen, Ransenna mumbled. It was clear to Idenno that she disliked this idea.

After Ransenna left the area, the Fire Queen turned toward Idenno. *Now, it's time to pick up where we left off yesterday.*

Where you left off, not me, Idenno said. *If you wish to earn anyone's respect, do not call the Leyrque's son a whelp.*

Why should I not call him what he is? The Fire Queen scowled. *It is clear that you will never respect me anyway, just as I can never respect an heir of Senbralni.*

If the Leyrque's son is a whelp, you are a whelp. You are the daughter of the former Leyrque Ammasan, after all.

The Fire Queen's eyes seemed to turn even more crimson as she spun quickly around and pinned Idenno's throat to the ground with her tail. If breathing was difficult before, this was agonizing. Iden gasped for air for what seemed like an eternity before she removed her tail.

I am not Ammasan's daughter! she shrieked. *I killed that foul Onizard with my own claws while your mother watched, screaming in agony.*

You speak as if she was a murdering demon like you instead of an innocent Child of Light.

She was a demon. She caused the death of innocence, the Fire Queen said as she shuddered. *But you wouldn't care about that, Heir of Senbralni. No, all you care about is your precious Rulsaesan and her family. You let your mother die and your brother suffer just to protect someone who didn't deserve that protection.*

Mekanni ordered me to protect both Rulsaesan and Deyraeno, Idenno said as, despite his urge to remain in control of as much of his body as possible, he shed a tear in remembrance of that terrible night. *You are the one who killed my mother and caused my brother and sister-in-law so much suffering. You are not going to put the guilt on me.*

So you deny that you abandoned your so-called love of your mother and brother for your pathetic one-sided lust for Rulsaesan?

I do, Idenno said. *I followed my brother's orders, and so prevented you from harming more innocents.*

Rulsaesan is not innocent either. Don't think I didn't notice how often she left the Sandleyr to talk to her honorable Watchzard. Then she named one of her sons after you. I have to wonder how many of those five children of hers were truly Deyraeno's children.

Rage filled Idenno's heart, and he managed to hit the Fire Queen with his tail before saying, *All of them were his children, you demon! My feelings of love for her were always there, and because I love her I could never interfere with her love for Deyraeno. Rulsaesan would never do that to him. I could never do that to him!* Iden shuddered in utter disgust. *Deyraeno and Rulsaesan are my friends!*

Some friends they were, the Fire Queen said, wincing and holding her tail to her side where she had been hit. *They didn't even argue when I made you Watchzard.*

Neither did I.

The Fire Queen scowled. *You fool! You are so calm, even as Rulsaesan abandons you, the heir of Senbralni, for an Onizard of lesser blood.*

Have you been talking to my grandfather or something? Such outdated views died with him.

Then why was Mekanni so upset when he thought the new heir of Senbralni was my child?

You fool. He was upset because you raped him, and he thought his only son was the child of a demon! I saw how desperately Mekanni wanted to have a child with Delsenni, and he thought that you made it impossible for him to ever have that child!

He could have had another child with Delsenni, the Fire Queen said. *She is his joinmate after all. I'm sure she would have consented.*

He can't do anything with her anymore, Idenno said. *He will always be haunted by the pain and trauma you put him through; it made him sick!*

I'm glad to know I had such a profound effect on him, the Fire Queen said as she smirked with terrible malice. *But now that the subject is being discussed, I'm curious. Tell me, do the other Onizards still believe that Delbralfi is mine?*

Of course not, Idenno scoffed. *Anyone with a mind could see that he was too much like his real mother to truly be yours.*

Then you just implied Rulsaesan is mindless. She was so convinced I had achieved my power through legal means, she was blind to the truth, the Fire Queen laughed. *If it weren't for Senraeno and that pathetic Bond of his, my plan would have been flawless.*

Flawless plans are meant to be foiled, and selfish hearts are meant to be broken, Idenno said.

As are foolish hearts and bones of my enemies, the Fire Queen replied. *Now it is time for me to enjoy myself more.*

Chapter 14

Ransenna shuddered. It was the screaming again. Though it was not as urgent as before, she could tell that whatever was happening to Idenno was just as terrible. It was clear that he was trying to protect Deldenno at some cost to himself. She did not want to know what that cost was; she feared that it would make her lose the last bit of dwindling hope she had left for their escape.

Once, when I was very young, Bral said I shouldn't trust you, Deldenno said. *Why would he say that?*

Ransenna blinked in surprise and shuddered. *I suppose it was because I used to work for that demon.*

You worked for the Fire Queen? Deldenno's eyes widened in apparent fear at this revelation. *Why would you do that?*

I was young, and stupid, Ransenna admitted. *I thought that by serving my queen, I would earn favor with important Onizards. I thought…no, I desperately wanted to believe that she was right about the humans, so I ignored the screams of the humans she killed. I wondered to myself why it should even matter. I thought they were just…animals.* At this, Ransenna burst into tears. *Oh, there were times when I believed that what I was doing was utterly wrong, but I let her convince me that I was in the right. I gave in like a stupid coward.*

What changed your mind? Obviously you're a different Onizard today, for you hate the Fire Queen.

I may hate her, but I am still a coward for not fighting her.

You seem strong enough to me. You made the right decision; we are all still alive, thanks to you.

I appreciate your confidence, Ransenna said. *In answer to your original question, I was converted on the brink of death. If you remember, I was Invited to your hatching ceremony. When your brother Delculble hatched, we became Bonds. But something went wrong; we were separated, and the Leyr Grounds began to flood.*

Bral was worried about the rain, Deldenno said. *That's all I really remember about what happened after we Bonded.*

He had every right to be worried. That was a terrible storm, and it only got worse after you left the Leyr Grounds. It was bad enough to convince the Fire Queen that your brother and Jena could have died in the chaos. I couldn't find Delculble, and he was drowning in the floodwaters!

It hurt so much, to think the one being who saw good in me was going to die, and I couldn't do anything about it! But then I saw something utterly strange; a human girl carrying my Delculble, saving him from the floodwaters at the risk of her own life. To think, I owed my life to a creature that I had believed was a mere animal. I would not have rescued her if the situation was reversed; she seemed to know this, and she rescued Delculble anyway.

Zarder Jena is a very special person, Deldenno said.

She is, Ransenna agreed. *I am glad she made that choice, for it was then that I vowed to stop working for the Fire Queen. I could not support someone who would lie to us all and keep innocents as slaves, killing them at will. I tried to free my own slave, but she just reassigned him to another Onizard. I hope he is alright; he was old, and she may have spotted his weaknesses.*

Deldenno smiled and said, *Now I see why Bral didn't trust you. But I don't agree with him. Delculble isn't the only Onizard who sees good in you; I see good in you as well.*

Ransenna looked into his grey eyes and smiled back. *Thank you, Deldenno. You should get some sleep now; the Lord of the Sky knows when your next opportunity for sleep will be.*

You sleep well, too, he said before he yawned and closed his eyes.

It wasn't until after he fell asleep that Ransenna realized the screaming had stopped. Nervously, she turned around and saw the Fire Queen staring at her.

How much did you hear? she asked, hiding her fear as best as she could.

I heard enough to know you left out a vital part of the story, the Fire Queen said. *The poor lad will hate you when he knows the full truth.*

That is a truth that only I can tell him.

I agree, the Fire Queen said as she smirked at Ransenna and the sleeping Child of Water. *I won't spoil the surprise for him. It will be much more amusing to watch his reaction as you say it. And you will say it before this is over; I'm not letting such a gem of a story be hidden. I still say, though, that you could have been a great Onizard if you listened to me.*

I'd rather not be your version of a great Onizard. What you wanted me to do was unspeakable.

Deldenno will believe your feelings were unspeakable, the Fire Queen said as she walked off, leaving Ransenna to tremble in fear.

The Child of Earth wished the Lord of the Sky's greatest plague would visit the Fire Queen for reminding her of that dark secret of her past. She couldn't tell Deldenno her secret now; he probably wouldn't hate her, but she did not want to see the disappointment in his eyes. After a long time waiting and watching for the Fire Queen's return, Ransenna finally allowed herself to go to sleep.

Chapter 15

By the time Bryn had buried the last of the bodies, the daylight was rapidly disappearing. The task had been utterly grim, especially since it was difficult to tell which parts belonged to which individual. Each of the bodies had been charred beyond recognition.

Amazingly, the little girl had not really cried throughout the process of finding the seeds. She had made comments about which trees were the favorites of various people, but she did not cry. Bryn could tell that she was holding back her emotions, for the girl looked as if she had been absolutely crushed. But what could Bryn say? He was certain the phrase 'I'm sorry your entire family is dead' would not have gone over well.

"May He who created the earth use you to renew it," Delma whispered, carefully moving dirt over the last seed she had planted. Now there was a line of dirt mounds where she had planted the trees over the graves. Finally, she began to sob as the last of the sun's rays disappeared.

Bryn sighed and said, "We shouldn't stay here for the night. We must respect the dead and let them rest in peace."

Where do you suggest we go? Xolt asked. *I'm not going to be able to see to fly any further, and I don't want to go back to the Sandleyr. Can you imagine the scolding we'll get from Leyrkan Mekanni?*

"No, we can't go back," Bryn said. "I don't want to say good-bye to Jena a second time. It would stress her out too much."

We can't let that happen, and we can't risk our lives by trying to fly further. You're supposed to return and take care of your child, Xolt said. *I don't think Jena would appreciate raising a child on her own. I know Erfasfi and I were pains to our mom and dad when we were that young.*

"Add in not being able to talk, the tendency to spit up food, the frequent soiling of clothes, and constant crying. Then you might be able to get the idea," Bryn said, resisting the urge to smile at Xolt's reaction of terror. "We can go to the training grounds and rest there for the night. I know I would appreciate being able to get a clear view of the stars."

"What are the training grounds?" Delma asked as she lifted her head from the patch of earth where she had planted the last of the trees.

They are where I learned how to fly, Xolt said. *We passed them coming here.*

"That area with the hill and all that short grass?" Delma asked. "I wondered where that hill could have come from."

"Apparently it was built when the Sandleyr was," Bryn said. "Onizards are pretty talented when it comes to that kind of stuff."

"The grass is soft there. It would be a good place to sleep."

"Yes, it would," Bryn said. "Let's walk there."

"Mister Bryn, I don't think I can walk anymore," Delma said as she attempted to get up, then stumbled. "I'm too tired…"

Then I can carry you, said Xolt as he picked her up and placed her on his back.

The two Bonds walked the distance to the training grounds before they both sat down near the hill. It was only after they stayed silent for a moment that they heard the voice of an Onizard speaking to the stars.

Lord of the Sky, protect them all. Don't let them feel the pain I've suffered. Let them live to enjoy their lives. May they not see death or feel the pain of defeat.

By this time, Bryn recognized the voice of Mekanni. Glancing toward Xolt, he shared a look with his Bond. They were trying to tell each other the same thing: let him be. He obviously worked hard to be alone, if Delsenni wasn't here. Leyrkan Mekanni hardly went anywhere without his joinmate; they were like two pieces of a clam shell, nearly inseparable and unable to live without the other half.

Lord of the Sky, if they must suffer, let them live to learn of the joys of life. Please, let them live, Mekanni said. Bryn thought he heard the Onizard sobbing, but he did not want this to be true. Mekanni had always seemed so strong, so in control when he wasn't sick. Without Delsenni to protect him, would he go mad there as Bryn and Xolt helplessly watched? *But if they must die, give us all the strength to carry on their memories. You've already given me so many memories to carry. Sometimes I wonder if Mesenni chose the right Onizard to be his heir. I know my sickness causes needless pain to others, but I hope that the joy I have given Delsenni makes up for it. I thank you for sending her to me, for giving me the strength to love her when all other strengths fail. I pray that you will give the same strength to Bryn as he is separated from his Jena.*

Bryn blinked in surprise. From what Jena had told him of the events leading up to the defeat of the Fire Queen, the strength of Mekanni was something to be greatly respected. He wasn't certain he could live up to such high standards of love and devotion. Then again, he had challenged the Fire Queen out of love for Jena before, and he would do so again. Perhaps Mekanni's prayer would not go unanswered.

And please protect Xoltorble. He is young and strong, but he does not know what may lie ahead of him. His family loves him very much, and would not like to see him get hurt.

Bryn resisted the urge to laugh as he watched Xolt cringe at both his full name and the implications of what Mekanni had said. Xolt hated it when people implied he'd get hurt easily, even though it was partially true. When he was a hatchling, Xolt was the clumsiest Onizard in the Sandleyr; many children of Earth could tell stories of how they'd healed Xolt after he made some silly error in judgment while using his powers of speed.

You've made Idenno strong, but he is facing his greatest challenge yet. Please give him the strength and courage to protect those he loves. Don't let the eyes take him. Mekanni sighed and paused for a moment before continuing with, *I am sorry I have not talked to you in a while; I have spent too long justifying excuses for delaying it. But I thank you for the blessings I have received from you, and leave everything to you. I know that everything happens for a reason; I just hope that someday I will understand that reason.*

Mekanni hobbled down the hill on his good legs and started walking toward the path. The Leyrkan of Night paused for a moment. *I know Bryn and Xoltorble can't hear me, but let them know that they are loved. Thank you, Lord of the Sky,* he said before he walked down the path and disappeared from vision.

He saw us, didn't he, Bryn? Xolt asked once his grandfather was gone.

"Of course he did. Leyrkan Mekanni isn't stupid." Bryn said. After a moment of thought, he laughed. "He probably sensed us there the whole time. It seems strange that he didn't speak to us directly."

At least he didn't yell at us the way he yelled at us during training, Xolt said. *That really hurt my feelings when he did that.*

"It may have hurt your feelings, but it made you stronger," Bryn said. "Feelings can be repaired far more easily than broken strength."

That's true, Xolt said, before he yawned. *Good night, Bryn.*

"Good night, Xolt," Bryn said. He watched his Bond fall asleep, but before he drifted off to sweet dreams of Jena, he said a prayer of his own.

Chapter 16

Idenno awakened and saw nothing but the crimson eyes of the Fire Queen glaring at him with intense, unchanging hatred. He would have jumped back in alarm if he was able to move at all. As it was, his tail was broken, and if he wasn't careful, his legs would be broken soon. He needed to keep those intact for when the time was right.

Did you rest well? The Fire Queen said in a mocking tone that was a bad impersonation of Ransenna's voice.

I have no choice but to say I didn't, Idenno said. *You obviously don't want me to rest at all.*

I never said that, she said. *I need you alive until I kill Senraeno.*

Why are you so obsessed with killing Senraeno? He showed you mercy and let you go free when he should have just killed you right there.

That is exactly why I must kill him, explained the Fire Queen. *He left me alive to suffer my humiliation and defeat, to watch a non-nature become a Child of Light. I saw Rulsaesan, one of my greatest enemies, become the Leyrque, taking my place as ruler of the Day Kingdom. I have roamed this wilderness for six years, having nothing to amuse myself but killing stupid humans. Where is the challenge in that? What is my purpose in living now, other than to be some high-handed, moralistic story for the Sandleyr?*

Idenno frowned as he angrily listened to this justification the Fire Queen gave to her deeds. *You would blame Senraeno for allowing you to be punished by staying alive? It is not his fault you are a murderer of innocents who still received mercy.*

The Fire Queen laughed loudly, and an occasional small flame came from her mouth as she laughed too hard to control it. *I am not blaming Senraeno for allowing me to be punished. I am blaming him for not punishing me. I deserve to die for what I've done; I have no delusions about that, and no regrets about it either. However, as long as my enemies are merciful weaklings, they deserve to die for being too weak to do what must be done.*

Then you actually want to die?

Yes, the Fire Queen admitted. *But I refuse to kill myself, and no one will fight to kill as I do. Senraeno will come soon, and he will die in his turn, for he is just as foolish and arrogant as you.*

Idenno shook his head. *It seems your greatest weakness is your suicidal pride. Senraeno will come, and he will defeat you.*

We shall see, Watchzard Idenno, the Fire Queen said as she stepped away from him. *It seems that your greatest weakness is your lust for Rulsaesan.*

I do not lust for Rulsaesan, Idenno said, angry that the topic had changed to his love again. It was getting rather aggravating, even if it was a delay that was giving Senraeno more time to catch up with them. *Rulsaesan is my true love.*

True love? The Fire Queen shook her head as she scowled. *That is rather ridiculous talk, considering she does not claim to love you in return.*

If that is what you believe true love is, I do not believe in your definition of true love, Idenno said. *That implies that those who love as I have done for the past twenty years love falsely and blindly. I cannot believe that. I believe in love returned and love unreturned, but not true love as others see it. That is for nonsensical stories we are told when we are young.*

The Fire Queen turned back toward him and grinned. *Ah, but love itself is a nonsensical story we are told when we are young. At best, it controls the lustful urges of Onizards. At worst, it is a dangerous lie told to protect the reigns of the Children of Light. I would bet that if Rulsaesan suddenly became haggard and repulsively ugly, you would drop such strong urge to protect her.*

I would if I lusted after her. But I do not; I love her, and I will continue to love her as long as I am capable of loving her.

You may not love her for long, then, the Fire Queen said, *for as soon as Senraeno comes, you will watch as he dies, and then you will die under my claws in your turn.*

If that is my fate, so be it, Idenno said.

The Fire Queen stared at him as if she were completely confused. *Why are you so calm about your fate? I could easily tell Ransenna not to heal you, and let you suffer in agony before you finally die.*

Then do it, Idenno said calmly.
What did you just say?
Do it, Idenno repeated slowly. *Let me suffer in agony. But first let me know why you even care*

about the fate of an insignificant Watchzard. I know you had some ulterior motive for wanting to kill every last one of the Children of Light, and I know you harmed my brother in some vain attempt to prove that his child with Delsenni was your own. I even understand why you want to murder Senraeno, even if I don't agree with your logic. Why do you choose me as an object to vent your hatred on?

If you do not know, you are a pathetic fool, the Fire Queen said.

Idenno frowned. *If I ignored the reasoning behind your utter madness, then you'd have the right to call me a fool. But you haven't told me what your reason for hating me is. Since you plan on killing me soon, I at least have the right to know the truth.*

You only have the right to know what I tell you, the Fire Queen said as she finally lifted him onto her back. *Ransenna, it is time to go!*

Fire Queen, Idenno still needs to be healed! The Child of Earth said.

Silence! The Fire Queen turned toward Ransenna, hitting Idenno with her tail in the process. *I have not given you permission to heal him, have I?*

No, Fire Queen, Ransenna said as she backed away timidly.

Then pick up your charge and follow me! The Fire Queen shouted.

The last thing Idenno saw before he fell asleep again was what appeared to be a large blur of blue and black on the landscape below. Was he actually seeing things correctly, or was the pain from his injury starting to mess with his mind even more? Idenno decided it was the injury, and prayed that it would stop bothering him soon.

Chapter 17

Blue trees? Ransenna asked Deldenno. *Am I seeing them correctly?*

Blue flowers on black trees, Deldenno said. *If that is what you see, I see them too. They'd be rather beautiful if the day wasn't so dark and depressing.*

At least we have each other and Idenno, Ransenna said. *We'll get through this.*

When you say it, I could almost believe you, The Child of Water said. From the tone of his voice, Ransenna could sense he was smiling.

Ransenna thought back to the previous night and frowned. *Deldenno, can I ask you something?*

Of course, but first I must ask you something, he said.

What is it you wish to ask?

Don't call me Deldenno; it makes you sound like my mother. All of my friends call me Delden, and if we have any chance of surviving at all, I'd like to survive as friends, if you don't mind.

Of course I don't mind, Ransenna said as she grinned. *I would be honored to be your friend.*

After a moment of silence, Deldenno said, *You had a question, I believe.*

It was not really a question. It was more of a request, Ransenna said. *As your friend, I must warn you that the Fire Queen is excellent at telling half-truths and outright lies to Onizards.*

Everyone knows that. She fooled my Bond into thinking he was her son for ten years.

She also told half-truths about me, Ransenna said. *My first love stopped speaking to me because she told him wretched lies about me. Of course, I did not know she had done this until it was too late. I think she wanted me to devote my time to working for her instead of spending time with him.*

That is terrible! Deldenno said. Then, after Ransenna stayed silent, he added, *First love? So you love someone else now?* His tone was hesitant, almost fearful.

Perhaps, Ransenna said, inwardly worrying that he had figured out the truth about her crush on him. *But I could not say it in front of him. After what happened, I swore to myself that I would be more careful about that sort of thing.*

At the expense of the one you love?

Well, no. If it was a life or death situation, I would not hesitate to tell him the truth. But the way our society is, most males appreciate the ladies letting them be the one to first say such things.

I don't know where you got that idea from, Deldenno said as he shook his head.

It's the truth, Ransenna said. *Take a look at all of the recent couples. Bryn was the first one to tell Jena. He was so obvious with that whole "brightest star in the heavens" sentimentality. Your Bond told Teltresan, indeed the entire Sandleyr, when he thought she was dying. Why, if a lady were to tell a gentleman of her feelings, she'd be considered...a white goose among wild geese. She just wouldn't belong.*

Now that's utter nonsense, Deldenno said. *My mother was the first to tell my father of her feelings, and she's Leyrque now. Bral told Teltresan while she was unconscious, but then he turned timid when she woke up, and she had to tell him in front of the entire Sandleyr. My brother told me that Jena didn't actually know for certain that Bryn's feelings for her were romantic until she told him that she loved him. From what I understand, Delsenni was the first to tell Mekanni, and no one can doubt the strength of their relationship. As far as I'm concerned, as long as she and I end up happy together, I don't care who is the first to get the courage to admit the truth.*

That is fine for them, Ransenna said. *But I'd still need time to work up the courage. What happened in the past was difficult, and it hurt me deeply. It took me years to recover from it, and I'm still scared of what could happen if I let my emotions take control.*

Everyone fears that, Deldenno said. *It is a part of life. But do not let the fear rule your life, my friend.*

I will not, Ransenna said, though privately she knew she still did.

Chapter 18

This looks like a good place to spend the night, Xolt said as he looked at the landscape below him. While everything always looked much better from the air, it seemed that this particular location would still be decent upon landing. There was a river running through the forest, and a nice green glade that would be perfect for a landing spot. Though it did not seem big enough for an Onizard like the Fire Queen, the glade appeared large enough for a Child of Wind like Xolt to land safely.

"The water looks clean," Delma said. "It seems nice enough, though I don't recognize this place."

"Things look different in the air. Perhaps you will recognize it once we reach the ground," Bryn said. "Okay, Xolt, we can rest here. Just be careful going in. I don't want to end up wrestling with a tree."

Why not? I always win when I wrestle trees, Xolt said, turning his head and grinning as he teased his Bond.

"Mister Xolt, you're gonna crash!" Delma screamed.

Sorry, Xolt said as he returned to looking where he was going. That was probably a good idea, though he wasn't going to admit it to the young human.

After he circled the glade a few times, he carefully glided in and landed gently on the grass. In retrospect, it was probably not such a good idea to land near a river when the size of his landing spot was unknown; Xolt slipped on the bank and nearly dropped his passengers into the river.

There's barely enough room for me to stand, Xolt whined.

"We'll deal with that as best as we can," Bryn said. "It's nearly sundown, and I don't want you to fly blindly in the dark. We'll lose our sense of direction if we do that."

"Mister Bryn and I can sleep next to trees," Delma said. "Roots make good headrests."

"Compared to what, the ground?" Bryn asked.

"Well, yeah." Delma said. "I thought that was obvious."

"You have to keep in mind that I haven't been out in the wilderness since I was younger than you. I have no idea what I'm doing."

"You mean you don't know how to find food or how to sleep or anything?" Delma asked. Xolt thought she was staring at Bryn as if he were a foolish non-nature, and it upset him.

"Well…no," Bryn said.

I can live off this grass, Xolt said. *It's not like the sea oats at home, but there's plenty of it.*

"I'm sure there's food for…mushrooms!" Delma exclaimed, happily pointing toward several white things sticking up from the ground by the trees.

"We don't need food for mushrooms, whatever they are," Bryn said. "We need human food."

"Mushrooms are human food!" Delma said. "They're really good, unless you get the kind that kill you."

"Oh, great," Bryn said as he walked over to the cluster of mushrooms, inspecting each one. He attempted to pick one, only to earn Delma's frantic screaming.

"No! Mister Bryn, don't eat that! That'll kill you!"

"How can you even tell which kind will kill you?" Bryn asked, fearfully tossing that particular mushroom aside.

"If you don't fall down dead, you ate the good kind," Delma said.

"That's very reassuring," Bryn said.

"But I can tell the difference!" Delma said as she wandered to the mushrooms and stared at them for a few moments. "These ones all look good." She said, pointing to a particular group that Bryn had missed previously.

"Are you sure?"

"Sure," Delma said as she picked one of the mushrooms and began eating. "They're delicious."

If you say so, Xolt said as he backed up slightly, then sat down. *I'm going to stick with the grass.*

The two humans proceeded to eat the mushrooms one by one. When Delma ate the last mushroom near them, Bryn wandered to another cluster and grabbed a mushroom.

"These really are quite delicious," Bryn said.

"I told you so!" Delma exclaimed. "See, I can help you guys."

"You certainly can," Bryn said. "Thank you for introducing me to the good mushrooms."

After they were finished eating, the three rescuers attempted to fall asleep as they watched the sun set over the trees. But Xolt noticed that Bryn was not going to sleep well, even taking the tree root pillows into consideration; he kept jumping after apparently seeing something in the woods.

Bryn? Xolt asked, extending his Bond's name by several seconds. There was something strange going on; Xolt could not sense the stable mind of Bryn from his end of their link. Bryn was there, and yet he was not; it was almost as if he were sleeping and awake at the same time.

"I'm going to go investigate that," Bryn said as he stood up and started walking toward the forest.

Investigate what, Bryn? Can't it wait until morning?

"No!" Bryn shouted. "There are blue Onizacs invading! Fly, Xolt!"

What? Xolt asked. But it was too late; Bryn had already run into the woods.

"What's wrong with Mister Bryn?" Delma asked as she rose to her feet, rubbing her eyes.

I don't know, Xolt cried. *He's seeing stuff that isn't there, and now he's run away!*

"Stuff that isn't there?" Delma asked, narrowing her eyes as she stared at the ground. "Did he eat some of those mushrooms right there?"

I think so, Xolt said cautiously.

"He ate them? Only Crazy Gréog ate that stuff!"

Crazy Gréog?

"Yeah, Crazy Gréog ate those mushrooms all the time. That's what made him crazy."

What! Bryn's going crazy? It's not permanent, is it?

93

"No," Delma said calmly. "Crazy Gréog would wander around for a while, claim to see strange things, make up stories about old guys bothering people going to weddings, and throw up a lot. My aunt always said that he was dumb for eating stuff that made him throw up, but Mommy said Crazy Gréog was just sad his family was gone," Delma paused for a moment and frowned. "I'm not gonna eat those mushrooms, though."

Good for you, Xolt said, trying to hide his irritation at the situation. *Throwing up doesn't hurt, does it?*

"Mommy and Daddy wouldn't let me listen to Gréog afterward. I think he said bad words."

Stars, Bryn is going to say bad words, too. And so will I, since I have to feel his pain.

"You feel his pain?" Delma asked, slowly stating each word as if she didn't believe Xolt.

Yes, we are Bonds, Xolt said. *I am connected to him, and he is connected to me. When he dies, I will die.*

"It's a good thing he didn't eat one of the bad mushrooms, then. Now all we need to do is find him."

He ran into the woods! I can't go in there! If I accidentally knock down a tree onto him it would be a...a murder-suicide!

"But I can go into the woods. Don't worry, he won't be able to get very far. I just hope he doesn't start saying some boring story about dead birds like Gréog did sometimes. That one was the worst."

I just hope his story doesn't get too interesting.

Bryn stumbled along the forest floor, wincing each time a tree branch smacked him. The blue Onizacs were after him! It was a conspiracy! They were everywhere! Granted, the cats were harmless when you avoided the spike on the end of their tail, but they were still really annoying, especially when you couldn't hear their telepathic speech. When you couldn't hear them, they just sounded like they were squeaking when they talked, and they rarely let you hear them. Bryn had never heard any Onizacs speak other than Alair, the Onizac Bonded to Jena. These blue...no, green and pink Onizacs were more annoying than most.

"Bryn!" a recognizable voice called softly.

"Jena?" Bryn spun around and saw his wife smiling at him in all of her beauty. Granted, he didn't remember her hair being dark green, but he had heard pregnancy messed with the emotions of women, so it was possible her emotions got the better of her hair.

"Oh, Bryn!" Jena said softly, half-moaning his name. "You're so strong and handsome. Come kiss me!"

"In front of the Onizacs?" Bryn asked. They had decided to be purple now, and it was a nice shade for them.

"Yes, you silly man who I absolutely adore," Jena said as she motioned for him to come closer. "If you really loved me, you'll kiss me now."

Several of the Onizac squeaks sounded suspiciously like laughter, but Bryn was willing to ignore that for the sake of a kiss from Jena. Granted, she sounded like she had been possessed by a bad romantic story, but Bryn wasn't going to complain about that. The colors were too pretty.

Bryn slowly moved toward Jena; she did not move at all, but smiled at him and waited for him to make the first move. He grasped her rough, coarse body and kissed her dry lips. Since when did Jena have a rough, coarse body and dry lips? That was certainly odd.

"Jena, what happened to your lips?" Bryn asked. But Jena had disappeared, and his arms were around a pink and yellow tree.

"Mister Bryn loves a tree!" Delma said as she started to giggle hysterically, running back toward the glade.

"I do not!" Bryn shouted as he stumbled forward after her. "I love Jena!"

"Mister Bryn loves a tree named Jena!" Delma shouted.

Bryn felt utterly ill and stupid. He was never going to live that down. On the bright side, at least the glade and Xolt were a comforting shade of blue that reminded him of Senraeno and his strength. After throwing up the "food" Delma had suggested, Bryn staggered toward Xolt and fell to the ground, letting dreams of the real Jena fill his head.

Chapter 19

Jena is a fool if she thinks she can win, the Fire Queen said the next morning. *Where I am taking you, the grass grows tall for miles, and it is dry after a long drought. One simple use of my powers, and the entire grassland will go up in flames. I made certain of that before I drove those pathetic humans toward you.*

Why did you kill them? Idenno asked. *You could have set a fire to the forest itself and brought us there to put a stop to it.*

And miss a perfectly good chance to practice my skills at ridding the world of the weaker species? The Fire Queen shook her head. *Never. Besides, they were only humans.*

Perhaps you forget that not everyone agrees with you on that subject, Idenno said. *If I recall correctly, two humans have challenged you and lived.*

Those two humans were lucky weaklings, the Fire Queen said as she frowned. *I knocked Jena unconscious, and I could have killed her if I had not decided to gloat.*

What about Bryn? You could never harm him.

Rulsaesan rescued Senme, and he's probably gotten himself killed from his own loud-mouthed stupidity.

Actually, he's alive and happily married.

A pity, the Fire Queen said. *While I don't advocate the reproduction of the human race in general, I especially despise the idea of that idiotic human reproducing.*

I'm sure he despises the idea of you reproducing a thousand times more, Idenno said.

He is Delbralfi's friend, is he not?

Ah, but as I have already clearly told you, your lie has been exposed. Everyone in the Sandleyr knows now that Delsenni is his true mother.

A great pity indeed, the Fire Queen said. *I shall just have to produce a new heir.*

You think it's that simple? Idenno asked. *You can't just take some unwilling male, have your way with him, and thus produce an heir. They may be an heir of your body, but not an heir of your mind.*

You say that only because you have no heirs, the Fire Queen shook her head and laughed. *Unless there's something we weren't told about Deldenno.*

Deldenno is Deyraeno's son, Idenno said firmly.

Of course he is, the Fire Queen said. *I'm well aware of how easy it is to claim an egg is yours, and Rulsaesan was always willing to protect her dear Idenno.*

I am not her dear Idenno. Rulsaesan has chosen only Deyraeno, and I in turn have chosen no one.

The Fire Queen grinned. *Oh, this is even more precious. Imagine the shame when Deldenno hears some lie I tell him about his true father.*

Leave him out of this, Idenno shouted.

Perhaps I will, perhaps I won't, the Fire Queen said, staring toward the area where Ransenna and Deldenno were sleeping as if she were pondering the idea. *It will be bad for morale if I tell them now, and I need them to have hope enough to get to our final destination. After that, some bad morale may be useful.*

Then tell them what you did to me, Idenno said. *A lie about what happened in my past is irrelevant.*

Oh, but if I tell them that, I'll have to threaten to do that to them, the Fire Queen said. *And I prefer males my own age, thank you very much.*

You're not welcome.

Ah, but you have no control over that, the Fire Queen said as she stepped closer to Idenno. *You cannot stop me; until Senraeno comes or you die, you won't have control over your own body. I own you.*

You may think you own my body, Idenno said. *But you will never own my heart.*

Why should I care? I don't need your heart to enjoy myself, the Fire Queen scoffed. *In fact, hearts are nothing more than nuisances, telling you what your lusts are. If I didn't need the energy to carry you, I would put you in your place right now.*

And you think that scares me? Idenno asked, laughing loudly until the pain from his wound overwhelmed him. *I have heard you kill my mother and torment my brother to the point where he is no longer of sane mind. I saw your tortures from afar as I served Rulsaesan as Watchzard-*

You served me as Watchzard, the Fire Queen corrected.

I never served you, Idenno said. *Did you not consider that the information from an Onizard who watches everything might be useful to the rightful*

Leyrque of the Sandleyr? Did you not wonder why I accepted that position so readily, so calmly?

You were promised a release of your lusts, the Fire Queen said as she grinned.

I was promised nothing! Rulsaesan needed help, and I aided her as best as I could, because I am her friend, and I love her. I realize you don't believe in that concept, but I do. I have felt it and seen it, and I know that it will defeat you in the end.

We shall see, the Fire Queen said. *In the meantime, you are forbidden the healing from Ransenna until you admit that love does not exist.*

Then I will die to prove you wrong, if it comes to that, Idenno said. *I do not think you will let me die on my own, though. You are going to kill me with your own claws, because it would disgust you to think that you had not chosen the time of my death.*

Chapter 20

Ransenna woke up and cautiously healed a portion of Deldenno's wing wound before she stepped toward Idenno. She did not see the Fire Queen around, but that did not mean she was not there. She could just as easily be hiding behind her, waiting for her to make some sort of mistake.

Lord Idenno, are you awake? She asked. When he did not move, she nervously added, *Are you alive?*

Yes, of course, Idenno said. *Your exceptional abilities have seen to that. However, I am tired, and every time I move, I am in pain. Unfortunately, the Fire Queen has forbidden you from healing me today.*

But you're very ill! Ransenna said. *And doubtless she's been doing other things to you. Your tail looks mangled, and you've been screaming every night that we've been hostages.*

You can hear that? Idenno asked, lifting his head slightly before he apparently gave up in that attempt. *I had hoped Deldenno wouldn't hear that.*

He assumes that you are just screaming due to your injuries, Ransenna said. *I hope there is nothing more to it than that.*

I am just screaming due to injuries, Idenno said as he closed his eyes. *That's all Deldenno needs to know.*

Ransenna could sense there was far more to this situation than he was revealing, but she knew she would get no answer from him. If her suspicions were correct about the trauma to his body, there was no way that Idenno would admit anything, especially since he thought by concealing his pain he was protecting an Onizard he saw as a son he never had. No matter; she did not need to know the details, and neither did Deldenno.

Indeed, the Fire Queen said as she knocked down a tree in her path. *What happens between Idenno and I is my own business. Go take care of the whelp. We are moving out.*

Yes, Fire Queen, Ransenna said as she quickly backed away. At first she thought the Fire Queen was reading her mind, until she realized that the Fire Queen was responding to Idenno's comment.

You are not to speak unless spoken to, the Fire Queen said, not looking at either of the Onizards.

Ransenna assumed the Fire Queen meant Idenno, but she wasn't certain. After she paused for a moment, she walked back to Delden and gently picked him up before she took off after the Fire Queen.

You saw my Uncle Iden? Delden asked.

I did, Ransenna said.

How is he?

Ransenna winced and desperately searched her mind for some lie. While her father had taught her to never lie about an Onizard's physical condition, she knew she had no choice in the matter now. *He's doing well, given the circumstances.*

Granted, I'd rather have him back at the Sandleyr with a better healer, but he'll live.

A better healer than you? Delden asked incredulously.

I am a young Onizard still, Ransenna said. *I still have much to learn about being a proper Child of Earth.*

I'd imagine being out here is a great learning experience, then, Delden said. *I myself am learning a great deal about lying on the ground all day and letting pretty women carry me around.*

Hopefully that won't spoil you, Ransenna said as she laughed. She was rather glad that Delden could not see her blushing.

Oh, it won't. I'm perfectly aware that this is a temporary situation, and when I get back to the Sandleyr, I'll be ignored by pretty women again.

Not necessarily, Ransenna said. *How do you know they all ignore you?*

I've seen them hovering around Bral, Delden said as he laughed. Ransenna had to carefully maneuver so he would not fall off her back mid-air. *Then again, I'd rather be ignored by women that stupid.*

Hovering around Delbralfi? Ransenna blinked a few times from shock. *Don't they realize he's joinmated?*

Apparently they think they can turn him away from the light, Delden said. *But of course Teltresan is his love, and nothing could separate them.*

No one should ever try, Ransenna said. *When an Onizard obviously doesn't love someone, that someone shouldn't try to change their mind, especially when they're joinmated. It's utterly stupid, considering how obviously happy Delbralfi and Teltresan are.*

He's a father, and still they hover around him, Deldenno said. *I guess they admire his public speaking ability and his looks. I guess he's better looking than the other male Onizards, but I wouldn't know.*

Delbralfi has good looks and a good personality, but he certainly isn't the only Onizard with that combination, Ransenna said. *Besides, he is joinmated. If he looked at an Onizard other than Teltresan, I'd take back what I said about him having a good personality.*

If he looked at an Onizard other than Teltresan, I'd smack him myself. He's a lucky Onizard, and he knows it, Deldenno said as he sighed. *I hope I end up being that lucky someday.*

You never know when it comes to those things, Ransenna said as she inwardly cringed. He couldn't know about her feelings for him, could he? *The right Onizard for you is out there somewhere. You just need to find her.*

I don't believe in the true love, right woman for me nonsense, Deldenno said. *If that was true, there would be no unrequited love.*

Truthfully, I don't believe in it either, Ransenna said. *It's just a silly way of showing sympathy. I am sorry to have even brought it up.*

Well, I'm glad for your sympathy, Deldenno said. *And I am glad that I have you to talk to through this big mess I've gotten us into. I hope we all live through this.*

We will, Ransenna said calmly. *I have faith that we will.*

Chapter 21

"I am not eating a mushroom ever again," Bryn said when he woke up the next morning. His head hurt and he felt like he could barely stand up. Nevertheless, he managed to get up with Xolt's help.

"We can eat berries, then," Delma said. "Of course, I'll have to be the one to pick them; we can't trust you to find the right ones."

"Right ones?" Bryn asked, his voice betraying his weariness.

"Yeah. If you eat the wrong one, you die," Delma said. "And since you picked the crazy mushroom, you'll be dumb enough to pick the death berries."

Did you just call my Bond dumb? Xolt asked as he awakened, groggily glaring in the young girl's direction.

"Nope," Delma said as she quickly and forcefully shook her head. "Mister Bryn is smart, except when it comes to eating."

Oh, Xolt said. *I could have told you that.*

"Xolt! You're supposed to be on my side!" Bryn shouted.

No I'm not, Xolt said as he stood up. *I'm your Bond, not some parasitic extension of your mind.*

"Fine," Bryn said. "I'll remember not to argue for you when you and Erfasfi get in trouble again."

That's different, Xolt said. *Erfasfi is the one who is always getting into trouble. He's the childish one.*

"What's wrong with being a child?" Delma asked.

"Absolutely nothing is wrong with it, unless it's used as an excuse for bad behavior."

I'm not using it as an excuse, Xolt said. *I'm just saying that Erfasfi is the one who always gets us into trouble.*

"I understand that's what brothers are for," Bryn said.

"Nah, brothers are for protecting you," Delma said as she looked away. Bryn could tell that she was close to tears. "That's what my brother did, before…"

"I'm sure family won't stop protecting you, even when they aren't in the same place as you," Bryn explained. "That's another thing about family; they'll never disappear from your heart. Believe me, I've learned that the hard way."

"You've learned from the dragon taking your family, Mister Bryn?"

Bryn sighed. "I learned from the dragon taking the families from a lot of people. I was too young to really remember my father and mother, but I nearly lost all of the family that chose me. Jena had to pretend she was dead to protect herself, and Xolt's mom nearly got herself killed."

"The dragon kills Onizards too?" Delma asked, her eyes widening in surprise.

She can, Xolt said. *That's why we have to rescue the Onizards she kidnapped. We don't want our family to get taken as well.*

"Then we should go now," Delma said. "I don't want the dragon to hurt any more families."

I agree, Xolt said. *We've already wasted too much time here.*

"Are you sure you don't want to say goodbye, Mister Bryn?"

"Say goodbye to what?" he asked.

"To your tree," Delma said as if this were the obvious answer.

"No!" Bryn shouted.

You're not sure you don't want to say goodbye to the tree? Xolt asked as he snickered.

"I mean, yes!" Bryn shouted more fervently than before as he started to blush.

Xolt shook his head as he took off amidst Delma's nonstop giggling.

"Can we please not mention the tree anymore?" Bryn asked, inwardly groaning.

Actually, I find this story most amusing, Xolt said. *Tell me, how would you compare Jena to the fairest of trees?*

"You know I'd never do that willingly," Bryn said. "Jena is the fairest of all things, as far as I'm concerned, and that tree incident was an accident!"

"A funny accident," Delma said. "Mister Bryn loves a tree!"

"No I don't!" Bryn said. "It was the mushroom's fault!"

"Crazy Gréog said that too," Delma said. "Then he died."

"I'm not going to die, am I?" Bryn asked. "I don't want to die."

"You won't, silly." Delma said. "He died from burn wounds, not from mushrooms. He actually challenged the dragon one time."

"He did what?" Bryn asked. "How did he manage to stay alive long enough to blame a mushroom?"

"Easy," Delma said. "He jumped into a river."

Ah, that explains all, Xolt said. *Children of Fire can't stand water. Crazy Gréog was lucky.*

"He still died!"

Well, he was kinda lucky?

"He died in intense pain!"

Well, um... Xolt stammered. *At least he tried?*

Delma shook her head and sighed. "Yeah, he did. Too bad he couldn't swim."

"How did he manage to say those last words if he couldn't swim?"

Delma paused for a moment, and Bryn saw in her eyes the kind of fear a child gets when caught in the middle of an elaborate lie. "I think that was just something my aunt added in, now that you mention it."

"Very well," Bryn said. "The point is, I'm not going to die from eating that mushroom, am I?"

"No," Delma said. "You were lucky."

"Good," Bryn said. "I don't like the thought of imminent death."

"What's imminent mean?"

It means it's going to happen soon.

"Well, it won't be imminent until you find that dragon," Delma said.

"I hope not," Bryn said. "Our friends won't be happy if we die trying to rescue them."

I hope they're okay.

"I'm sure they are, Mister Xolt," Delma said. "You just got to believe they are."

I'll try, Xolt said. *It's just hard to keep faith out here.*

"No it isn't," Delma said. "Faith is strongest when you're afraid."

Chapter 22

Idenno walked about, looking at the Sandleyr as it slowly faded in around him. There was something wrong, and he could not quite understand what that was. Nothing was out of place, and the stars were quite bright in the night sky. Carefully he began to count them, when he realized that there were many more than there had ever been before. There had clearly been sort of massacre, and he had not been able to stop it.

Flying through the entrance, Idenno's worst fears were confirmed. There, strewn across the ground of the Invitation Hall like fallen trees, were the bodies of his family and friends. Some of them appeared to have died in their sleep. Others, like Deldenno and Senraeno, had their eyes wide open in terror. Their bodies were hopelessly mangled to the point of being almost unidentifiable. Mekanni and Delsenni had fallen side by side, though the Lady of Night had clearly fought much longer than Idenno's brother. Idenno tried to block the vision with his tears, but he could not hide from the painful scene. Everything was wrong.

Rulsaesan! Deyraeno! He shouted, desperate to find some sign of life. *Where are you?*

Delbralfi had fallen protecting Teltresan, and his blood mingled with hers on the ground. There was no fear in his eyes, only the shame of the last battle lost.

Rulsaesan! Idenno screamed.

He lost track of time as he searched; he could have been there for hours or mere minutes. But at last he found what was left of Rulsaesan and Deyraeno.

It seemed that she had died quickly; she was not awake to feel the suffering and the pain around her. Deyraeno had done his best to protect her, even as his great strength finally failed. But this was no comfort to Idenno; his love, his reason for living, was dead, and she had not had the chance to live the full and happy life that she deserved.

I've failed you, Idenno whispered as he began to cry over her body. *I failed you all.*

Idenno! Rulsaesan said in the calm but firm tone she reserved for serious situations.

Idenno lifted his head and saw Rulsaesan standing next to him. She was solid, unlike what he had heard about the spirits of Onizards. Suddenly, it was no longer night, and the carnage he had seen around him moments before had disappeared.

I am glad I found you. You were having a nightmare, Rulsaesan said.

Idenno took a few moments to regain his composure before he chuckled nervously. He was certain that this was the real Rulsaesan now; Children of Light had the power to enter the dreams of others. Delsenni had become the most proficient at this ability in her efforts to fight the Fire Queen, but Rulsaesan had played pranks of her own in her younger years as Lady of Day.

I am sure with your presence it is now a happy dream, Idenno replied as he bowed to her.

You silly Onizard, I'm in your head, Rulsaesan scolded. *There's no need to bow to me.*

Ah, but I do have reason to bow to you. You're Queen of my thoughts as well as Leyrque of the Sandleyr. You of all Onizards ought to know that.

I do, Rulsaesan said, *and I have always treasured the love from you that I cannot return. I am sorry you are in this terrible situation.*

The situation isn't that bad, Idenno said, hoping Rulsaesan wouldn't catch him in his lie. *Deldenno is safe under Ransenna's care.*

My son is growing up too quickly, Rulsaesan said as she shook her head.

So you've noticed his little crush as well? Idenno asked.

Of course, Rulsaesan said. *It's typical that everyone notices those things except the Onizard who is the object of the other's affections. Luckily for him, it seems that the affections are mutual.*

That is excellent news, Idenno said. *Now, all we need to do is get rescued.*

Help is coming, Rulsaesan said as she stared at the ground.

There's bad news, isn't there?

Well, it's not the help you expected, Rulsaesan said. *I don't want you to be disappointed about that. It is good help, but it is not Senraeno or Zarder Jena.*

Idenno sighed. *I should have known. The Sandleyr cannot risk its greatest hero to save the lowly Watchzard and the son of its Leyrque of Day.*

If I had any choice, Idenno, I would come to rescue you myself, Rulsaesan said as she scowled. Idenno could sense she was frustrated, for very briefly she faded from the dream. When she solidified again, she said, *Jena can't come, because she is with child. Zarder Bryn and Xoltorble are coming to rescue you.*

The fastest Onizard in the Sandleyr? Idenno said as he perked up for a moment. *But he's so innocent. How will he last in a long battle with the Fire Queen?*

Xoltorble and Bryn will distract the Fire Queen long enough for Ransenna to heal both of you, and then you can escape, Rulsaesan said.

I'm hurt pretty badly, Idenno admitted. *It will take precious time to heal me.*

I'm sure they'll be able to protect Ransenna when she heals you, Rulsaesan said as she began to fade away. *You are a strong Onizard, and one of my dearest friends. Stay strong, Idenno, and may the Lord of the Sky protect you.*

I will, Idenno said as he opened his eyes.

The pain of his wounds, hidden by his dreaming, returned to him. The harsh glare of the Fire Queen was not far away. But Idenno had hope again, for a good Onizard ruled the Day Kingdom.

You will what? the Fire Queen asked.

Continue to love Rulsaesan, and wait for the Zarder, Idenno replied, not caring what would happen to him in the short run of things. He had faith that the darkest of situations would improve.

Chapter 23

Deldenno awakened to the sound of Ransenna pacing about, checking his pulse and other vital clues to his general health. From the way she shook her head and smiled as he opened his eyes, he could tell that she was pleased he was able to awaken at all.

Did you have a good rest? she asked. From the way she glanced around, Deldenno could sense that she was afraid the conversation would be cut short.

Yes, Deldenno said as he stared at her eyes for a long moment. *A very pleasant rest.*

How unfortunate, the Fire Queen said as she stepped into view. *Ransenna! Stop dallying! We must reach the tall grass before nightfall!*

Yes, of course, she mumbled as she slowly set Deldenno on her back.

Deldenno could almost forget his pain, from the way she carefully carried him. All seemed right with the world, even considering the desperate situation. For a moment, even Idenno seemed full of hope as he shared a glance with Delden.

As Ransenna took off and began flying behind the Fire Queen, Deldenno said, *Last night, I dreamed my mother came and comforted me. She said that Idenno would protect us both.*

I had a similar dream, Ransenna said.

Your mother comforted you as well?

Well, no, Ransenna said quietly. *It was your mother who came and comforted me.*

Deldenno blinked. Something was clearly wrong, or else Ransenna's wings would not have tensed up underneath him. *Did I say something wrong?*

Well, no, it was a reasonable assumption. It's just that my mother died a long time ago.

I am sorry, Deldenno said. It upset him to think of hurting her, even unintentionally.

Oh, it is nothing to worry about, Ransenna said. *I don't really remember much about her. They say she was one of the kindest Children of Earth to have ever lived. The Great Lady Isenna; I constantly heard about her in my youth.*

If you don't mind me asking, how did she get that title? Deldenno asked. *I never heard about her.*

The Sandleyr has found greater heroes since then, Ransenna said. *In truth, if Teltresan had gained her powers as soon as Ammasan died, no one would have remembered her. From what I remember of the story, Isenna was a strong Child of Earth, but she used too much of her healing powers at once, and she collapsed and writhed in pain, as if she almost had the powers of a Child of Light for a few brief moments. She was never the same after that; she barely had enough strength to lay my egg. My father said that she lost all hope in the world.*

I am sorry, Ransenna, Deldenno said.

One night, a few months after I was born, she heard an Onizard screaming and went to investigate. He was badly injured, and his joinmate was sobbing, trying to get him the help he so desperately needed. Isenna obeyed the law to heal without prejudice, but she forgot to control her powers. She helped as much as she could, but her help cost her too much; the Onizard survived, but she collapsed and died a day later. That is why she was great; she sacrificed herself to help others, and died the death of a great Child of Earth. I have always hoped that I could someday follow in her footsteps.

Don't do that, Deldenno said.

Do what? Ransenna asked, her voice rising as if she were greatly offended. *Are you saying that I'm incapable of being a great Child of Earth?*

No, I am not saying that at all, Deldenno said quickly. *I think you're already a great Child of Earth. I just don't want you to die the death of a great Child of Earth. What would come of that other than pain for those around you?*

I think you greatly overestimate the amount of care those around me have for me, Ransenna said. *Though I wouldn't want to die; Delculble counts on me.*

Surely someone else cares about you, Ransenna, Deldenno said. He could think of one Onizard other than her Bond, but he would not admit it.

No, the Child of Earth said, *My father is dead too. Delculble is my only family.*

You have no family? Deldenno asked incredulously.

No. My father was an old Onizard when I was born, and he lived only long enough to see me become a full Child of Earth. But I still remember many things about him, like the goose story he told me.

I am terribly sorry, Ransenna. I am bringing up painful memories for you, when we should be focusing on something happy.

My father's memory is a happy one. I don't think I'd be the Onizard I am today if it wasn't for him.

Then I am thankful for him, Deldenno said. *I like the Onizard you are today. You're beautiful in all the ways you can be.*

You're overly flattering, Ransenna said. *I don't deserve that.*

Why not?

Well, for starters, no one else seems to think so. My first love didn't, at any rate.

Then your first love was an idiot! Deldenno exclaimed. *Tell me who he is, and I'll beat him up for you!* He added, only half-jokingly.

That won't be necessary, Ransenna said. *I'd rather not trouble other Children of Earth over him. Besides, I was stupid for falling for him in the first place.*

Nonsense, Deldenno said. *Love is not something to be ashamed of. Those who do not appreciate it are the ones who should be ashamed.*

I'll keep that in mind, Ransenna said, before she started concentrating more intently on the journey ahead of them. All was silent except for the beat of her wings upon the wind, and Delden found himself slowly drifting into an uneasy slumber.

Chapter 24

Bryn was utterly frustrated. Xolt had been flying all day at his fastest speed, and they had still not discovered the location of the missing Onizards. Bryn was beginning to doubt the girl's sense of direction; he was even starting to doubt the purpose of their quest. How was an inexperienced Onizard like Xolt supposed to find the Fire Queen in a world where every tree looked exactly the same?

"We've been traveling all this time, and there's still no sign of them," Bryn said. "What are we supposed to do?"

They had a good head start, Xolt said sadly. *They could be anywhere by now.*

"I know they're going north," Delma said firmly.

"How can you know that for certain?" Bryn asked.

"The dragon always came from the north when she attacked," Delma said. "We'd always manage to escape by watching the north for her to come. If she always came from the north, she'll always return to the north. It makes the most sense."

What is actually to the north, anyway? Xolt asked. *More trees?*

"No," Delma said. "There are fields of tall grass that stretch for miles and miles. If the dragon torched the fields, they will be black, but the grass is good for cooking when all else fails. I know...I knew many people who survived the winter by burning some of the tall grass to keep warm. It is a good place, but no one can go there anymore. It is the place of the dragon of fire."

Is the tall grass anything like sea oats? Xolt asked.

"I don't know what sea oats are."

Sea oats are golden brown plants that grow by the sea, Xolt explained. *It's what I normally eat. The Sandleyr has to grow them in abundance to feed all of the Onizards and humans that live in it.*

"The tall grass is golden brown," Delma said. "But there is no sea around it. There are a few caves, but not much else."

"That's probably what has kept the Fire Qu-I mean, the dragon alive, then," Bryn said. "As far as I'm aware, she doesn't actually eat anything she kills."

To do that would be an abomination, Xolt said.

"No more of an abomination than her other deeds," Bryn said. "But it doesn't matter. The point is, she has survived, and she is going to cause more pain until the day she dies."

"It's sad to think that the dragon could use something that was so pretty for such evil," Delma said. "I liked the tall grass until she came and ruined it for everyone."

"That is generally the way evil works," Bryn said.

Look! Xolt exclaimed. *There are two clearings ahead of us, both nearby each other. The grass is already flattened in four places.*

"Let's land and get a better look," Bryn said.

Xolt carefully glided to the ground and landed near one of the places in which the grass was flattened. When Bryn slid down his tail and got a closer look at the grass in question, he danced for joy.

"Look here! There's a place where the grass was burnt. The dragon was here. I'll bet that the other three patches of grass are where Deldenno, Idenno, and Ransenna slept that night."

It looks relatively fresh, Xolt said. *I'd guess they were here two days ago at the earliest. We're going the right way, Bryn! We have a greater hope of rescuing them now!*

"Guys, something is wrong," Delma said as she inspected the area.

"What is it?" Bryn asked as he walked toward her.

Delma looked up at him, frowning and looking as if she was about to cry. "There's dry blood here. One of them is hurt badly."

Bryn looked at the patch of grass she was looking at, and came to the same conclusion. "It must be Deldenno or Idenno. We knew that they were hurt, or else they would have escaped."

Ransenna is a Child of Earth, though, Xolt said. *She could heal them. She might have already healed them, for all we know.*

"Whoever it is needs to be home as soon as possible," Delma said.

Ransenna can look after him, Xolt said. *We're going as fast as we can; it's nearly nightfall now.*

"But we can still fly at night," Delma said. "You're fast, and strong. You can take a nap when this all is over, right Mister Bryn?"

Bryn sighed and paced about in thought for a few minutes. While he did not like this appearance of blood, he did not want to push Xolt to the breaking point before they even confronted the Fire Queen. "We should at least stay here for the night. Tomorrow, we fly at full speed to their rescue."

Chapter 25

We will stop now, The Fire Queen said. *We have arrived to the greatest area of my kingdom. We are at my home.*

Idenno stared at the blackened and barren ground below them. There was still plenty of tall grass to be found to the right of this area, and there were even a few patches among the blackened and barren ground where tall grass still grew, but they were few and far between. If this had been part of a prosperous field before, the Fire Queen had destroyed it. *A glorious place indeed. How do you expect to survive when the next rainstorm comes? You have no shelter here.*

The rain will not come for a while, the Fire Queen said. They dropped in altitude as she instinctively hid her tail flame underneath the rest of her body. *Besides, I have ample shelter. Of course, you cannot see it, for you are turned the wrong way. But no matter; just know that your beloved rainstorms cannot stop me.*

A pity, Idenno said.

Indeed, the Fire Queen said. *I've spoiled the surprise of it. I would have found it most amusing to see you dance that pathetic rain dance of yours in celebration of a victory, only to be burned to a crisp pile of bones when I choose to kill you.*

It sounds as if you have my death all planned out.

No, the Fire Queen said as she landed carefully on the ground. *I haven't decided how I will kill you yet,* she admitted, throwing Idenno down roughly.

Iden winced. A patch of tall grass had slightly lessened his fall, but some of that same tall grass had entered his wound. *It will be interesting to find out what you finally decide to do, though I don't know of many ways you could kill an Onizard.*

You have apparently not thought of the possibilities, the Fire Queen said as she shook her head. *I could simply cut your throat open, as I did with your mother. But I don't think you deserve something that quick; you've been a nuisance already, and you're bound to be even more of a nuisance before your end comes.*

So I'll die slowly, Idenno said. *Sounds like fun for your sadistic mind.*

The death of an enemy is not nearly as exciting as watching the enemy suffer, and I have thought of many possible ways to prolong your suffering. I could kill you by beating you to death, she said as she lifted her tail over Idenno's head. For a few moments, it seemed like she was carefully considering completing that method of annihilation without further delay. Then, she lowered her tail before continuing with, *That would not allow for much blood, though, and I want you to bleed. I want your heart to suffer as much as your body.*

Cut a million gashes into me, then? Idenno suggested.

And risk breaking one of my claws or my horn? No, the pain of the cuts would not last long, and bleeding to death does not take long either.

I've been bleeding to death for several days now, Idenno said, turning slowly to get the tall grass out of his wound and show the Fire Queen the severity of it at the same time.

No you haven't. Ransenna is keeping you alive.

Fine, then, Idenno said. *Ransenna is keeping me alive and suffering at the same time. Isn't that enough for you?*

No, the Fire Queen said. *It has to be pain enough to make you renounce Rulsaesan once and for all.*

Then you have a problem, for there is not pain enough to make me renounce Rulsaesan.

Really? the Fire Queen asked. *Already you are discussing your death with me, and you haven't mentioned Rulsaesan once before I brought the subject up.*

Why have you speak foul things about her when I can keep silent and gain strength as I think of her strength?

Strength? The Fire Queen laughed for a long time. *She had no strength when I ruled the Sandleyr.*

Idenno frowned. *You are wrong; Rulsaesan was among the strongest Onizards I ever knew. If you felt the pain from just one of your murders, you would crumble; Rulsaesan felt them all, and still stood tall. She even took the time to care about me, even as she loved Deyraeno.*

I'll bet that hurt poor, noble Idenno the most, to think he was not loved by his precious and dear Rulsaesan.

Idenno shook his head. *You'd lose that bet. I'd be lying if I said that it didn't hurt me a great deal to know I was not loved in return, but that is not what hurt me the most.*

I dare say, I'm curious now, the Fire Queen said as she smirked. *Tell me what hurt poor Idenno the most.*

What hurt me most, Idenno said, *was how each night she went to bed in pain from all the sadness in the Sandleyr. She never complained out loud about it, but those who knew and cared about her could see she was suffering. I stupidly thought that just by hiding my own pain, buy encouraging her to seek out her happiness at the expense of mine, I could help her.*

You failed her, then, the Fire Queen said, grinning with delight. *You admit disguising your lust by calling it love was useless.*

No, Idenno said, *for though I could not tell her the extent of my wishes for her happiness, that was not my duty. I've learned that now. Rulsaesan could never fully believe praise and well wishes from me, for I am unfairly biased in her favor. But she'd believe Deyraeno.*

I would think Deyraeno is more biased than you. He is her joinmate, after all.

No, not really, Idenno said, *but she has her bias toward him, and that makes his bias utterly precious, the most wonderful thing in the world. Though she appreciates what she cannot return, Rulsaesan cannot truly value my love in the same way she values Deyraeno's love. I would have it no other way.*

You would have her think your so-called love useless? The Fire Queen asked.

Yes, for it is, Idenno said. This thought brought him close to tears, but only for a moment. *My love is utterly useless to her. I cannot argue that. But I also cannot let go of my love. You'll never understand that, for you are incapable of love.*

So you say, the Fire Queen said. *I agree, only because love does not exist, only lusts and pathetic Watchzards who cannot look around and simply choose another Onizard as a mate.*

You think I have any care whatsoever about that? Idenno asked, shaking his head. *I do not. I know that I am not meant to be in a relationship with anyone. It would not be fair to Rulsaesan or the other lady for me to simply pretend my love for Rulsaesan has died.*

Our mothers certainly did just that, and they passed on their lines well enough, the Fire Queen said.

Idenno blinked a few times. *What are you talking about?*

Surely you've heard of the great, undying love of Ammafi and Senmafi, the Fire Queen said as she rolled her eyes. *They fell in love, despite the warnings of Lord Mesenni of Night. It was shameful, he said, for the last child of Senbralni to be involved with the same sex. A commoner of the same sex, even! It was utterly scandalous at the time, from what I was told.*

What does that have to do with anything? Idenno asked, his tone filled with anger. *The Sandleyr doesn't care about the gender of joinmates. Love is love.*

But Senmafi was destined to rule the Night Kingdom and produce heirs of Senbralni! the Fire Queen exclaimed, dramatically throwing her tail back and forth. *She could not be involved with another*

126

woman and produce those needed heirs! So, your mother became the joinmate of your father, and heartbroken Ammafi eventually became Ammasan, the joinmate of my father, Ranbralfi.

My father was never around, Idenno said. *I don't even know his full name.*

Of course not, the Fire Queen said. *He did not want the shame of being associated with your mother. He only wanted the honor of producing heirs of Senbralni.*

But there was no shame, Idenno said. *Mesenni was the only Onizard who found shame in that. My father was never around because he wanted to use my mother for his pleasure. Once he realized that he couldn't get much pleasure from her, he left her to raise us on her own. Mek and I swore we'd never be like him.*

You are wrong, the Fire Queen said. *Many found shame in that, for they could clearly see our mothers did not become joinmates out of love; they did so to please the lusts of their men. Once those lusts were dealt with, they simply resigned themselves to their unrequited lusts for each other. Didn't you ever wonder how I was able to find Leyrque Senmani so quickly after I killed my mother?*

Idenno shuddered from the cold way that the Fire Queen spoke of the murders she had committed. *The thought crossed my mind, but I prefer not to think about that night.*

Many nights, Senmani just stood there, watching my mother sleep. It happened with such disgusting regularity, I knew she would come again that night. So I waited to kill Ammasan until she was there. It was most amusing the way Senmani gave up the will to live. They should have just pleased their own lusts on each other, or else they should have given up those lusts.

You'd rather that neither you nor I ever existed?

Of course I'd rather not exist, the Fire Queen said. *Why live a useless existence of shame?*

Shame you brought upon yourself for becoming a demon, Idenno said.

No, the Fire Queen said as she glared at Idenno. *The children of Senbralni and the Children of Light shaped me into the demon I am today. It is your fault.*

Fine, blame me if you need to place the blame on someone, Idenno said. *This still doesn't explain why you want me to believe love doesn't exist.*

You are held back by your lusts, just as they were, the Fire Queen said. *If you simply gave up your pathetic lust for Rulsaesan, you could be a powerful Onizard. I could even help you gain your power, if you shared it with me.*

My love for her is power enough for me, Idenno said. *Even if it was not, I could never accept your help with anything. I refuse to associate myself with an unrepentant murderer.*

For a few moments, the Fire Queen seemed almost saddened by this statement. Then, once she regained her ability to speak, she said, *If you will not associate yourself with an Onizard who gave others what they deserved, then I will put you in your place. I will show you the fate of those who do not have the will to see the truth.*

Chapter 26

Deldenno could not see what was going on around him, for the sun was nearly gone, and the light was dim. He could see the light from the Fire Queen's tail flame a short distance away, but not much else. The beauty of Ransenna was barely visible, and not enough to protect him from the echoing screams of his friend Idenno.

I can't take this anymore! Deldenno screamed. *Something is wrong with Idenno! Can't you hear that screaming? He's hurt!*

We can't do anything about it, Ransenna said softly.

Deldenno scowled at the Child of Earth. *Yes we can! You could try healing him more than you are already healing him. Or better yet, you could heal me so I could fight off the Fire Queen!*

And risk both of our lives? Ransenna shuddered and avoided eye contact with him. *I can't do that, Delden. Please don't make this more difficult than it already is. I am already failing the Code of Earth for not completely healing him.*

Why can't you? Deldenno asked, unable to contain his frustration. *You keep saying that our lives are in danger, and you're using it as an excuse.*

Delbralfi helped Jena and Bryn at the risk of his own life, and you don't see him unhappy today.

Ransenna sighed and took several deep breaths. For a moment, it sounded like Deldenno had gone too far, and she was going to cry. Then she paused briefly before saying, *If I were to heal him more than I have been healing him, she would just hurt him more than she is hurting him already. I don't like the sound of this either, but there is nothing I can do. I wish I could switch places with you and be the injured Onizard. Then I wouldn't have to see the terrible injuries the Fire Queen is inflicting on him and deal with the knowledge that my healing powers are utterly useless. I want to help him; I want him to be free from this madness. But I'm helpless, Deldenno. I'm helpless and hopeless.*

Deldenno sighed and bit his lower lip. *You are not helpless or hopeless, Ransenna. You are stronger than you give yourself credit for. You'd have to be strong to carry my fat body all the way here.*

Ransenna emitted a laugh that mixed with a sob.

Ranse, don't lose hope. I am sorry that I lost control; I should not have gotten angry at you like that.

Ranse? she asked. She suppressed another sob as she stepped closer to him. *Where did that name come from?*

If I told you to call me Delden, I should be allowed to shorten your name as well. If that's acceptable to you, my friend.

Of course it is, she said. *It's just strange hearing a name like that again.*

Someone else has used that name for you?

My first love called me that a few times, Ransenna admitted. *It sounded odd coming from him, though. I like the way you say it much better.*

Why do you keep saying first love like that? Deldenno asked. *It sounds odd.*

Well, it's the truth, Ransenna said, sounding slightly annoyed by his comment. *He was the first Onizard I ever loved outside my family, but he was not the only Onizard I ever loved. So he's my first love, but not my last love. It feels more optimistic when I say it that way.*

Deldenno blinked a few times. *Uncle Iden says that once you love someone, you can't love again.*

Idenno is going by his own experience, but he is not the guiding example to everything. For most, love is eternal. But betrayal, hatred, and time can sometimes destroy love. You see, trust and respect are the crucial things that make love work, and if one or the other is destroyed, love cannot last.

Delden frowned and paused in thought. *So you're saying that you stopped trusting and respecting your first love, and you easily gave him up after that?*

I'm not saying it was easy giving him up, Ransenna said. *It was extremely difficult and painful for me. That was one of the darkest times in my life, for I could remember how grand it was to be in love with him while knowing that he greatly feared my love.*

He rejected you as a friend because he didn't return your love? Deldenno scowled in disgust. *What a monster!*

Oh, he still wanted to be friends with me, and I could not give up his friendship. But it was rather awkward after that. As soon as he heard some dreadful rumor about me, he dropped the friendship as quickly as possible, like it was the most worthless thing in the world.

The demon, Deldenno said. *If he's still around, I ought to smack him for you.*

That really isn't necessary, Ransenna said. *He's happy now, and I'm long over him. That is the way things should be.*

So you're happy alone?

I never said that, Ransenna said. *I'm just happy without him. Besides, I wouldn't be calling him my first love if I hadn't started to love someone else.*

Who is he? Deldenno asked.

Oh, Ransenna said. Her voice wavered, almost as if she were afraid to answer. *I'd rather not say right now. This is not the right place for such talk.*

Love does bring strength when all strength fails, Deldenno said. *It might be good for you to talk about it. Maybe if you start talking about it, I could find the courage to talk about it as well.*

I'd rather not, though, Ransenna said. *It's something I'd like to keep private for now, while I still can. The Fire Queen could use it against us.*

Suit yourself, Deldenno said as he sighed. She didn't get the hint at all. *I guess it'll be a discussion for another day, then.*

Have a good rest, Deldenno, Ransenna said. She gently healed more of his wound before she sat down nearby.

I'll try, he said as he closed his eyes. He knew that dreams of her would give him hope that night, but he could not find the words to say it.

Chapter 27

Bryn could not sleep, for the creatures of the night had apparently decided to throw a party he wasn't invited to. He had tried pacing about to force himself to go to sleep, but that wasn't doing anything but causing the random animal chatter to increase in volume. Xolt and Delma were having the same problem as Bryn, though they were channeling their insomnia in other ways.

"That's a whistler," Delma said in a matter-of-fact tone at the latest noise.

How can you tell that apart from the crikichin? Xolt asked.

"Easy," Delma said. "I listen, unlike you."

Well I'm sorry that you're closer to the ground and you can hear them better!

"Listen! It's a hoo bird!" Delma exclaimed as she danced about in what appeared to be a pointed effort to ignore Xolt.

"So, the point is?" Bryn asked. "It doesn't matter what they are. They're all just keeping us awake. This is ridiculous."

"No, it's great!" Delma said. "Usually the hoo birds fly away from humans. We're privileged to hear it."

"I'm flattered that they decided to keep us awake just for this evening," Bryn said. "Can't you tell it to be quiet with your brilliant nature skills?"

"I don't speak its language," Delma said. "Besides, it was here first. It didn't do anything to hurt anybody."

About this time, Bryn noticed movement in the grass nearby. A mouse lifted its head briefly, looked around, and froze. Before Bryn had time to blink, a strange winged creature swooped down from the tree, extended its sharp talons, and killed the mouse in an instant. The creature stared at Bryn, Delma, and Xolt with its large yellow eyes for a few moments before gracefully returning to the tree with the mouse carcass firmly in tow.

"It didn't do anything to hurt anybody?" Bryn asked carefully.

"It didn't do anything to hurt a human," Delma said. "Hoo birds have to eat too, you know."

It's disgusting, Xolt said. *The poor mouse didn't have a chance.*

"That's generally the way things work when it comes to eating," Bryn said. "She's right, though. The annoying creatures keeping us awake need to eat too."

"They are not annoying!" Delma said. "Hoo birds are pretty!"

Pretty creepy, if you ask me, Xolt said.

"That's not very nice," Delma said.

I'm not here to be nice. I'm here to attempt to sleep, which your hoo birds, crikichins, and whistlers are preventing at the moment.

"You could sleep if you wanted to," Delma said. "You just have to get used to their noises."

I notice you haven't gotten used to their noises yet, Xolt said.

"I'm used to their noises. I'm just not used to yours. You guys are making more noise than they are."

Technically I am not making any noise at all, since I speak telepathically.

"Yeah, but Bryn is," Delma said. "He's making all kinds of noise walking back and forth. It's probably why all the animals are talking so loudly."

"Great, once again my major problem is that I'm the subject of intense conversation," Bryn said as he sat down beside Xolt.

"At least people are talking about you," Delma said. "Hardly anybody ever notices me or wants to play with me."

You talk about Crazy Gréog all the time. How is that any better for him?

"True," Delma said, before she tilted her head. "Hey, what's that?" she asked, pointing toward a spot deeper into the woods.

Bryn turned and looked toward where it seemed she was pointing, and squinted. "I don't see anything."

"You're looking in the wrong place, silly. It's right there!"

Bryn blinked in surprise when he finally saw what Delma was talking about. The creature that Delma was indicating was pure white, and it had some sort of strange glow to it, as if it had come from the stars themselves. It appeared to be slightly taller than Bryn, and it stood on four legs. Instead of a tail it had long, fine hair that sparkled in the starlight. The same kind of hair also trailed down and almost covered its thick neck. It's long, proud head was lowered to the ground as it ate, and the horn on its head occasionally poked the ground below it.

"Wow, it's pretty," Delma whispered as she squinted to get a better look at it. "It's a unicorn! I never thought I'd see a unicorn. We should walk closer and get a better look at it."

Bryn, I don't think we should be bothering it, Xolt said. *It's a weird animal, and it's the same color as those mushrooms.*

"Don't be silly," Delma said. "Unicorns help travelers like us in times of need. Everyone who has ever heard the stories of them knows that. Maybe it will help us find our way toward the dragon, or it'll show us some secret place in the forest with really yummy berries and pretty flowers to make us happy before it tells us the secret to beating the dragon."

"Delma, can you really believe a story like that?"

"Of course!" the girl giggled. "Unicorn! Please help us!"

Startled by the loud, sudden noise, the unicorn lifted its head and stared at the trio.

Bryn, I don't like this, Xolt said, his voice shaking with nervousness.

"Delma, maybe we should go," Bryn said as he watched the unicorn carefully.

"But it's a unicorn!" Delma exclaimed before she started running toward it. "Please help us, Unicorn!"

The unicorn clearly did not want to help Delma. It snorted, pawed at the ground, and turned to face her, its ears lowering more by the second. By holding its head in front of its body, the unicorn made the horn a sharp object capable of impaling Delma.

The girl stopped and stared. "I'm sorry." She whispered as she started to back away.

The unicorn pawed at the ground a few more times before it charged toward her, still holding its head in front of its body.

"Mister Bryn! Xolt! Help me!" Delma screamed.

I told you so, Xolt said, turning his head toward the unicorn and glaring at it. His head provided ample protection for Delma once she ran behind it.

The unicorn nearly stumbled as it attempted to force all of its legs to come to a stop at once. Its ears fell back even further as it reared in surprise, then turned and ran in the opposite direction. As it ran, a smaller unicorn appeared from behind a nearby thicket and started running with the taller one. Soon they had disappeared into the forest.

"Oh," Delma said as she cautiously peered at the departing unicorns. "It had a baby. I forgot."

How could you forget something you didn't know? Xolt asked.

"No, I forgot the rest of the story. Unicorns help travelers in times of need, unless they have a baby. Then they kill travelers or anything in the area that looks like trouble."

"Smart creatures," Bryn said. "When it comes to protecting children, they're just like every other creature in existence."

"No, sometimes animals eat their babies, and sometimes they just leave them behind and don't even care. They're not always protective."

"Then they're just like every other good creature in existence."

"But all animals are good," Delma protested.

"Fine," Bryn said, and his sleep deprivation was evident in his tone of voice. "They're just like every other creature that is protective of its children."

"That's much better!" Delma said.

Well, everything seems to have quieted down, so can we all please go to sleep now? Xolt asked.

"Of course," Bryn said as he finally closed his eyes. He only hoped that the others were getting rest as well, or at least finding comfort somehow.

Chapter 28

Idenno was pretending to be asleep, but he had one eye open to view the stars. He felt almost guilty looking at them, for he had not truly studied them since he stopped dwelling in the Night Kingdom. There were many new stars in the sky since he had grown up; he wondered how many of them belonged to those he knew, and he feared that some of them could have been prevented if he had just been more diligent as Watchzard.

The Fire Queen was actually sleeping now; at least, her breathing sounded like an Onizard in deep sleep. He didn't want to risk finding out she was awake by moving to a more comfortable position. His side was aching tremendously, and the night was much colder than the previous nights he had spent in the wilderness. If the Fire Queen's tail flame had not been nearby, Iden knew he would have frozen there. But Iden would never say this; owing his life to a demon didn't make any sense.

The chill of the night only made the stars seem brighter and more real to Idenno. Each star seemed to glisten with the coldness of death, imprisoned in the bleak, black night sky. Each star was a champion of light, an Onizard or human who had done well in life and brought the love in their hearts with them through death. These were heroes, the innocents who had led good lives who now were examples to others.

Yet even as they gave him hope, the stars seemed cruel and selfish to Idenno. Why keep your love to yourself, even if you were already dead and anyone alive had forgotten it? Keeping his love for Rulsaesan to himself had nearly cost Iden his friendship with Rulsaesan and Deyraeno, and he had vowed not to hide it anymore. What good would being a star be if those he cared about forgot that he loved them? But there was nothing he could do about it; all good Onizard became stars at death. He only wished that it didn't seem so much like a trap and a restriction.

To Iden, the rain was a better representation of love; as it fell without care for itself, it renewed life around it. One drop of rain might not seem to matter much in the course of the storm, but that raindrop might feed the crops that kept an Onizard alive. Others complained about the rain, but Idenno could not; to him, it was utterly precious, more precious than the stars, even though it did not contain the souls of the dead.

The Fire Queen yawned and stretched before turning in Idenno's direction. Her eyes were now open; Idenno attempted to shut his before she saw that he was awake.

It won't work, you fool, the Fire Queen said. *I can tell by the way you're shuddering that you acknowledge my presence. You don't have to fear me, you know.*

How are you so certain that I fear you? Idenno asked. *I'm just shivering from the cold.*

Oh please, don't lie to me. Your eyes are turning more lavender than usual. That has always been a trait of heirs of Senbralni when they are afraid.

That is utterly insane. Our eyes also turn lavender when we are sad, and they can stay lavender permanently if the stress is great enough. My eyes have stayed lavender ever since I learned Rulsaesan didn't love me in return.

Poor baby, the Fire Queen said as she rolled her eyes. *The point remains that you do not have to be afraid of me. I won't kill you until I am done with you.*

I am not afraid of you or anything you can do to me.

Good. Then perhaps we can simply talk.

Talk? Idenno asked incredulously. *There is nothing you can say that I want to hear.*

But I want to hear more about your past, the Fire Queen said. *What made you decide to leave the Night Kingdom, where you were respected, to pursue the affections of the mere commoner Rulsaena? Even when she became Rulsaesan, she was still of less than noble blood. An heir of Senbralni deserves so much better than that.*

What is with your nonsensical fixation on noble blood? Even if I am the direct descendant of Senbralni from parent to child over the generations, someone had to choose an Onizard of lesser blood in order to produce me. Heirs of Senbralni couldn't very well choose to be incestuous.

Though the idea is appealing, the Fire Queen said as she grinned.

You disgusting monster! Have you no morals?

No, I do not have morals. I have no need for them; I know who I am without the guidelines dictated by those who claim to be better than me.

Morals are not something dictated by those who claim to be better than you. They are what inspire you to be a better person in the first place, Idenno said.

A better person to whom? the Fire Queen asked. *Why should I care, when no one will even see me after you are all dead?*

You should still aspire to be a better person for yourself, Idenno said.

Myself? I hate myself, the Fire Queen scoffed. *Enjoy the cold, foolish Watchzard. You still have much to learn before I kill you.*

You are the one who needs to learn, Idenno said softly, ignoring the chill of the night as he concentrated on thoughts of Rulsaesan.

Chapter 29

Ransenna shivered from the cold. She was glad that she didn't hear any screaming, for it allowed Deldenno to get the rest that he needed, and it at least told her that Idenno's injuries weren't getting any worse. The stars were a comfort to her, but knowing that those under her care were not suffering from something she could prevent was much more reassuring to her.

Ranse, you look cold, Deldenno said softly.

Ransenna nearly jumped in surprise. *You're supposed to be asleep, silly goose. How can you get well when you don't rest to recover your strength?*

My friend is cold, and so am I, Deldenno said. *I can't sleep with those two concerns on my mind. Besides, it's a beautiful night; I'd like to enjoy beauty while I still can.*

I suppose there's no shame in that, Ransenna said, shaking her head as she sighed. *Which star is your favorite?*

What? Deldenno asked.

Well, you said you wanted to enjoy beauty, so I assumed you meant the stars, Ransenna explained, feeling embarrassed for having incorrectly guessed Deldenno's intentions.

Well, I didn't, Deldenno said as he started to grin. *I said I wanted to enjoy beauty, and I meant it. I can't concentrate on the stars; they're all the same, and once you realize you're just staring at a bunch of dead people, they become grim. But you, Ranse, are beautiful, both inside and out.*

Ransenna began to blush. *Thank you, Delden. You are too.*

I'm beautiful? Deldenno asked, laughing until he cringed, apparently from the side of his wings hurting again.

Well, no. Ransenna stammered. *I mean yes. I mean…you know what I meant.*

Of course. I was only teasing, Deldenno said. *Maybe we'll both blush so much that we'll warm ourselves up and forget the cold.*

Maybe, Ransenna said. *At least, your company is a blessed thing for me. I'm glad that you're such a good friend to me.*

And I'm glad you're such a good friend to me, Deldenno said, before he cringed once again.

Your burns are acting up again, aren't they? Ransenna asked as she lifted her tail to place it on his side. *Let me just heal-*

No, don't risk it, Ranse, Deldenno began, lifting up his own tail in an attempt to block her.

The tips of their tails touched together, sending shivers down Ransenna's spine. She didn't want to let her feelings for him effect her so greatly, and yet when she slowly looked into his eyes, she could not help but be overwhelmed by emotion. He truly cared about her; he was not simply befriending her because he needed her healing powers to survive. And as she thought about it more, Ransenna realized that she cared about him too. She was not dealing with a mere crush anymore; she loved him.

Now don't be silly, Ransenna said as she forced herself to move her tail, losing that brief connection with him. She gave him her healing touch, but it was not enough; she could only prevent some of his pain, and she wanted to protect him from all of it. *If you're hurt, I'm going to help you. If you need me, I am here for you. I am your friend, and that is what friends are for.*

I am glad that you are my friend, Deldenno said. *I just don't want to lose you.*

And I don't want to lose you. So you need to rest and recover your strength, Delden.

Ranse? he asked, his tone seeming to reflect concern, fear, and nervousness.

Yes, Delden?

*If it is alright with you, could we...*he trailed off as he frowned, as if struggling to find the right words. *It's still cold, and I don't want you to freeze. Could we...I mean, not wanting to disrespect you, but could we...*

Sleep side by side? Ransenna asked, amazed but happy from the suggestion.

Deldenno sighed and smiled as if a heavy burden was lifted off of him. *Well, yes. As long as we have no other way to keep warm, I thought it would be a good idea. Not wanting to disrespect or dishonor you, of course.*

I would not want to disrespect or dishonor you, my friend, Ransenna said as she sat down close beside him. *But you are right; the world is cold, and we have each other for warmth. I will help you rest.*

Deldenno smiled as he drifted off to sleep. Ransenna did her best to control her rapidly beating heart, but it was difficult, especially in his unconscious state he wrapped his tail around her. Feeling as though she were grinning like an idiot,

Ransenna forgot the cold and her fear of the future. Whatever happened, she had her dear friend for comfort.

Chapter 30

Bryn shivered from the cold. They had chosen a good landing spot this time, with plenty of room for Xolt to walk about. But the chill that had come in had crushed the triumph of finding this location. Bryn was not dressed for the weather, and neither was Delma, though she seemed to be faring better than Bryn was.

This is horrid, Xolt said. *It reminds me of that story Grandma Senni used to tell me about the cold night when they missed talking to Jena. This chill could have sent Grandpa Mek over the edge.*

"It could have," Bryn said. "But it won't send us over the edge. Grandpa Mek had Grandma Senni, and we have each other."

"That's not really that much," Delma said.

"Yes it is," Bryn said. "Xolt and I are family. With us looking after each other and you, we should be fine. The cold weather cannot last forever."

"It lasts a long time," Delma said. "And it makes me sad. When I was little, I used to listen to my mommy and daddy sing songs about the past, and it gave me hope. But my mommy and daddy are gone now; what am I supposed to do?"

"Write your own songs," Bryn said. "I'm sure your parents deserve their own song, and you are the only one who can sing it."

"What'll I sing about them?" Delma asked. "I'm not talented at all. I can't sing."

"Just sing the good things that you remember about them," Bryn said. "Maybe it'll help you take your mind off the weather as you think of those you care about."

"Who do you think about, Mister Bryn?" Delma asked. "Not trees, I hope."

Xolt laughed and shook his head. *Nah, he and the tree had a nasty break-up.*

Bryn glared in his Bond's direction as he said, "No, I don't think about trees."

"Then who do you think about, Mister Bryn?"

Bryn smiled, for he had thought the answer was obvious. "My wife, Zarder Jena. She is my strength, there is no question about it. When we were young, I was almost scared of her, but as I grew older, I realized her strength was what I loved most about her. When I thought she was dead, I called her the brightest star in the heavens, but the truth is that they don't compare to her."

"You should sing about her, Mister Bryn!" Delma exclaimed as she giggled.

Him? Sing? You must be out of your mind! Xolt said. *I know Onizards who could sing better than he can.*

"Can Onizards even sing?" Delma asked.

No, Xolt said. *Which is precisely the point. Bryn couldn't sing if he wanted to sing.*

"I wanna hear now!" Delma said, turning toward Bryn and grinning eagerly.

"Xolt's right, I can't sing," Bryn said. "I wouldn't do her justice with my singing voice."

"So? My mom and dad wouldn't want me to sing about them either. C'mon, I wanna hear you sing!"

Bryn sighed and shook his head. "Some other time, Delma. Right now, I feel almost as bad as I did in the half year when I thought she was dead. I couldn't even sing a song of the worst quality."

"I'm sorry, Mister Bryn," Delma said. "Thinking about people you love is hard sometimes, isn't it?"

"It is," Bryn agreed. "But it is what makes us worthy of the stars."

It's time we all went to sleep, Xolt said softly. *We'll need rest for tomorrow. The Lord of the Sky only knows what odd things will happen to us then.*

Chapter 31

Idenno could sense that something strange was going on. Not only had the Fire Queen avoided trying to use him for her pleasure, she had stopped talking to him as well. Idenno had not even seen her all day. He certainly was not complaining; it was a welcome relief, but it seemed as if she were waiting, planning some new and more terrible torture for him. Perhaps her sudden disappearance was only an attempt to make him go insane, waiting for her to strike again.

Idenno, Ransenna said as she stepped toward him. *We must hurry. I will heal you, and you can escape.*

You shouldn't be wasting your powers on me, Idenno said. *Use your strength to help Deldenno.*

You know he would never try to escape without you.

That is foolish, Idenno said. *What good will I be alive if he dies? He's the Bond of Delbralfi, who is joinmate to Lady Teltresan. The entire Sandleyr depends on him remaining alive. Besides, I think you'd rather keep him alive than me.*

It is my job to heal without prejudice, giving preference to those who have the worst wound. Ransenna said evenly.

Now don't start talking like Teltrena the non-nature, Idenno said. *You'd be more wounded if Deldenno died then if I died. Just admit it.*

Well, yes, Ransenna said quietly. *I would.*

Then say it to him. Don't wait until he's dead to say your life revolves around him.

If the Fire Queen finds out-

She'll do what? Kill you? Idenno shook his head. *She can't, not when the Zarder is coming to rescue us.*

Do you really think that Zarder Jena is going to miraculously come and rescue us?

No. I think the Zarder will come at the opportune moment. There's no miracle about that; it's a fact.

How do you know that?

Rulsaesan told me in a dream, Idenno said.

That's quite encouraging, Ransenna said as she sighed. *We should all just live on our dreams, then?*

If the dreams give an important message, then yes, Idenno said. *I'd trust Rulsaesan with my life.*

Why? Ransenna asked. *She's a good Leyrque, but not worth that kind of protection.*

When you love someone, that person is most definitely worth that kind of protection, Idenno said.

Don't put silly ideas into the girl's head, Idenno, the Fire Queen said as she emerged from the tall grass and walked very slowly back to them.

Idenno blinked a few times, certain that he was not seeing correctly. Why was the Fire Queen wincing each time she took a step or moved her tail? Surely there was nothing in this area that could have injured her, and certainly nothing that could make the Fire Queen wince! But something had apparently struggled with her for a long time, for she was breathing more heavily than usual. From the way her breaths were paced, it sounded as if she was attempting to mask that, but she was failing, and it confused Idenno greatly. The former Watchzard wished he knew what had caused her such pain, so he could ally himself with that creature or object.

Ransenna apparently saw this strange and sudden weakness as well, for her eyes widened in shock and she gasped as she stepped away.

What is wrong, Ransenna? The Fire Queen asked. *Caught in some silly escape plan? Be glad that Idenno did not agree with you, for I would have killed you both if you had tried to escape.*

I am sorry, Fire Queen, Ransenna said, lowering her head. *I thought-*

There is your problem, the Fire Queen said. *You thought. Once you start thinking, you start thinking of foolish things. Go take care of Deldenno.*

But, Fire Queen, Ransenna protested. *Idenno is still injured. He needs healing.*

If he truly needs it, and I decide to let him live a while longer, I will shout for you, the Fire Queen said in a tone that made her sound more irritated than normal. *Go away!*

Ransenna quickly moved away, but not before glancing back a few times as she ran through to the other side of the tall grass.

Foolish child, the Fire Queen said. *She still thinks she's doing good by healing the dead.*

And you still think you're doing good by killing your enemies, Idenno said.

You can't tell me you wouldn't kill me if you had the chance.

I can tell you it would be very tempting, Idenno said after a moment's thought. *But if*

Rulsaesan told me not to kill you, I would not kill you.

Will you stop talking about your most perfect lady, the infallible Leyrque Rulsaesan? The Fire Queen shouted, turning toward Idenno and scowling as if she were dealing with a frustrating child who would not listen to reason. *You act as if you're some sort of noble martyr for lusting after someone who doesn't return your lusts. It is not as if you are the first to deal with that situation, and you won't be the last.*

And you know everything there is to know about it, Idenno said as he rolled his eyes and turned his head away from her.

I do, the Fire Queen said, lifting his head with her tail and staring at him directly in the eyes. Idenno had heard stories of the terrible, emotionless glare of the Fire Queen, but it did not have the impact he expected. It was terrifying in its own way, of course; Iden could never deny that. But at the same time, it seemed as if she were hiding some inner turmoil, and that her emotionless eyes were only that way because she was afraid of any emotions. Iden could have almost had sympathy for her, if not for the fact that she was a demon who was planning to kill him like she'd killed his mother.

Really? Idenno asked, ignoring for the moment the threat of her tail flame so near his hair and ear. *How did you get to be the expert?*

Do you think I spent ten years ruling the Sandleyr without seeing the terrible effects that believing in love had on Onizards who could have been strong? Lady Delsenni could have easily defeated me and created the Sandleyr she wanted, but her so-called love for Mekanni and the idiot that they spawned kept her from using her full strength. She had to hide behind that pathetic hatchling Senraeno when she could have easily defeated me herself. I would have preferred a match between equals far more than a match with a hatchling and a non-nature.

Which you lost, said Idenno.

I lost that match only because I was unprepared. Senraeno did not give me the courtesy to inform me he had gained his powers. I at least give my enemies the opportunity to fight back and then suffer the full agony and defeat of death. Senraeno did not even offer me the courtesy of dying when I asked him to kill me. I would have at least let him realize the pain just in time for his pain to end completely. I was going to be merciful, but now I will offer only revenge.

You have no right to speak of mercy when you have murdered innocent Onizards in their sleep! Idenno shouted.

Innocent? The Fire Queen began to laugh as she set Idenno's head back onto the ground. *Ammasan was hardly innocent. She who was supposed to promote the myth of love was one of the first Onizards to reveal it for the lust that it was. She claimed to love Senmafi, but she took my father as a joinmate anyway. She simply chose the more convenient lust for her political gain, and then abandoned him once raising me was no longer a problem.*

Then she was wrong, Idenno said.

What? The Fire Queen blinked a few times and stared at him for a moment.

She was wrong, Idenno said. *You were wrong for killing her, and she was wrong for denying her love. Delsenni would have been wrong if she had denied her love; it is simple as that.*

But if we all just admit it is nothing but lust, the world will be a better place, the Fire Queen said. *How many fools have made themselves into martyrs over the lack of a simple act of pleasure? How many have been happier once they realized that this thing you call love is something they can control for their benefit?*

That is not love, Idenno said. *What you describe is lust.*

Exactly, the Fire Queen said, stepping closer to Idenno as she smiled, moving her tail over his body. *I knew you were a sensible Onizard I could convince of the truth.*

Idenno shuddered and tried to shake her off. *You misunderstand me. What you describe is lust, but that does not mean love does not exist. I agree with you that they are fools if they think that lust is actually love. I will be the first to yell at them if I find out that is their belief system. Love is not about the benefit of the individual, or some fleeting moments of pleasure followed by rejection and humiliation. Love is caring so much about someone that you would do anything just to ensure their happiness.*

You cannot completely ensure anyone's happiness, the Fire Queen said. *They can pretend to be cheerful, but they won't truly be happy all of the time.*

Of course they won't, Idenno said. *That is an unrealistic goal. But when you love someone, you want to make sure they are as happy as they possibly can be. If you can see they are happier without you, then you give them their space, and cut your losses. If they are happy with you, and love you in return, then it is the most wonderful feeling in the world, from what I understand.*

That is utterly foolish, the Fire Queen said. *If this emotion exists, it will only bring down the capable Onizards to the level of the ones they love.*

Of course you think it's foolish. You have not experienced love for anything other than yourself or your power, Idenno said. *But those who have ever loved in their life know that it is not foolish. You claim that it only brings down the capable Onizards, but it actually lifts them up. If Delsenni had not had Mekanni's love in all her trials and tribulations, I don't think she could have survived the insane emotional turmoil you put her through for taking her child.*

She could have survived, if she had seen it for the lust that it was, and simply developed her own strength instead of letting her belief in love cloud her judgments, the Fire Queen said. *Protecting a child made her utterly weak; it was just something that came from her body. Why did she need to worry about another lustful Onizard coming into the world? She was happy enough without him.*

If you were ever a real parent instead of a kidnapping monster, you would think differently, Idenno said. *You spoke of Delsenni making the Sandleyr she wanted, but the only way she could do that would be to raise a child with her ideals.*

Really? the Fire Queen asked as she shook her head and rolled her eyes. *It is good, then, that you will not be able to raise any heirs of Senbralni. The Sandleyr will be better off without your ideals.*

I have heirs, though not of my own body, Idenno said. *That is enough for me.*

You will not have heirs, when I finally kill you and your precious Deldenno, The Fire Queen said. *Why are you so content to not have children of your own? Does your lust for Rulsaesan blind you so much as to not want your bloodline to survive for future generations? Do you not desire children at all?*

No, my love for her does not blind me. I did want children once, but not at the cost of someone else, Idenno said. *There are more important things than mere procreation.*

Like what? The Fire Queen asked.

The dignity of others, Idenno said. *Something you will never understand.*

Chapter 32

Ransenna shuddered as she completed the walk back to Deldenno. While she was glad that the Fire Queen was weakened at the moment, her idea of why the Fire Queen was weakened made that thought no joy to her. Ransenna had many questions about the day's events, and none of them had any good answers. Where had the Fire Queen been for so long, and how much had she heard of the conversation? Was Idenno paying for her escape plan now? Or was the Fire Queen slowly taunting him with malicious words and threats of things to come?

Ransenna could not mention these fears to Deldenno, though. She did not want him to worry as she was worrying. He had a much greater connection to Idenno than she did, and fears of Idenno's pain would make Deldenno's pain much worse. Deldenno needed to keep his dignity, in spite of his inability to defend himself.

Ranse, Deldenno asked, *How is Uncle Iden?*

He is fine, Ransenna said. *How are you?*

All the more better for having you here, Deldenno said. *Did you hear any news of the Zarder coming?*

No, Ransenna admitted, *but the Fire Queen is weakening. When I saw her, she was changed somehow. She didn't seem to be at her full strength. If the Zarder comes within the next few days, she'll catch the Fire Queen in this weakness.*

That is excellent news! Deldenno exclaimed. *Uncle Iden will probably discover what is causing her weakness and exploit it. He can tell the Zarder, and the Fire Queen will be defeated for good! Of course, that leaves one question; what are we to do in the meantime?*

Wait, and talk to each other, Ransenna said. *It's all we really can do.*

Then maybe you can answer a question I have, Ranse, Deldenno said.

What might that be? Ransenna asked.

When you said that you had a second love…um…who is he?

Ransenna blinked in surprise and terror. *I'm not really ready to answer that; my feelings for him are so new, I barely understand them myself. But I know I'm in love; I have no doubts about that.*

When will you be ready to say that to him? Deldenno asked.

When the time is right, I guess, Ransenna said. *Feelings like love need to be given the respect and dignity of time. I don't want to simply blurt it out.*

Why not? Deldenno asked.

Well, I don't think you would, if you were in love, Ransenna said. *You'd find her too marvelous to simply say it outright. You'd want to show it in other ways first.*

Of course, Deldenno agreed. *But there is such thing as too much time. Delbralfi was almost too late to tell Teltresan of his feelings; I don't want to make his mistake.*

Then you're in love? Ransenna asked, her heart filling with hope.

Of course not, the Fire Queen said as she stomped by them. Her glare was much more powerful than before, and it seemed that she was recovering from whatever had weakened her before. *Love does not exist. You ought to know that, Ransenna; what you thought was everlasting love has died before.*

I only thought it was everlasting love because I was young and stupid, Ransenna said. *I loved in my past, but sometimes love is not meant to be. And other times it is; you have no right to judge what is love and what is not, for you are incapable of loving anyone but yourself.*

I warn you, Ransenna, that I am in an extremely bad mood, the Fire Queen said. *Do not tempt me to kill you now.*

I am sorry, Ransenna said. *I have the right to my opinion, and you have the right to yours.*

My opinion is more powerful when with one breath I could kill both of you, the Fire Queen said as she turned away from them. *But since I need to preserve my strength for Senraeno, I will leave you be for now. Don't get yourselves into trouble.*

After the Fire Queen left, Deldenno blinked in confusion a few times. *Don't get yourselves into trouble? That sounds like something my mother would say.*

It sounds like what any mother would say to two adult Onizards of the opposite gender, Ransenna said. Then, after she realized a different possibility, she added, *Sometimes a mother will say that to two adult Onizards of the same gender as well.*

What does she think we're planning on doing? Deldenno asked. *It's not like we're joinmates or anything.*

That doesn't matter to the Fire Queen, Ransenna said as she shuddered. *She thinks that such activities should not be restricted to joinmates.*

Well, that's utter nonsense, Deldenno said. *Then again, I should have known that. She didn't mind the talk about her when everyone thought that Bral was the son of her and some random non-nature.*

She probably enjoyed it, Ransenna said. Then, after an awkward silence, she asked, *So, what was your answer to my question?*

Which question?

The one that I asked before the Fire Queen so rudely interrupted.

Deldenno blinked a few times and then started laughing. *I don't remember what the question was. Could you repeat it for me?*

Ransenna grinned from embarrassment as she started to blush. *I asked you if you were in love.*

Deldenno's face turned a distinct shade of crimson. *Yes,* he mumbled, deliberately looking away from Ransenna.

May I ask who? Ransenna asked.

You can, but I can't answer. Not now, Delden said. After he sighed deeply, he added, *I want to say it, of course. I want to shout it so everyone in the Sandleyr can hear it. But I'm a scared hypocrite.*

You don't have to be scared of telling me. I won't tell anyone else, Ransenna said.

I'm not, Deldenno said. *I'm definitely not scared of telling you. I'm scared of what the Fire Queen could do if she found out my weakness.*

Ransenna nodded and sighed; it was true that the Fire Queen would probably hurt them both if she found out that Ransenna loved Delden. If he loved her in return, it would be both a blessing and a curse.

I will tell you, Ranse, Delden said. *But not right now. We must wait for the right moment.*

Of course, Ransenna said. *When you are ready, I will listen. In the meantime, this is just another reason to hope the Zarder is slowly getting closer.*

Chapter 33

"This looks like a good place to stop," Bryn said as he surveyed the area below them. He was exhausted, and the sun was slowly fading away. Xolt was showing signs of fatigue as well; his wings were not beating as quickly, and he was slowly sinking closer to the ground. They had made good progress that day, but that would be no consolation if they crashed to the ground and died.

There are blue trees everywhere, Xolt said. *How am I supposed to land?*

"You're small; you'll find a way," Bryn said.

"Small?" Delma exclaimed. "Xolt's huge!"

Apparently you haven't met Deyraeno, Xolt said. *I'm actually among the smallest of the Onizards. But I make up for it by being among the most agile.*

"Then you'll have no problem landing amongst those trees," Bryn said. "Aren't you the least bit curious about blue trees?"

Curiousity killed the Onizard stupid enough to fly into a blue tree, Xolt said.

"There's an area there that doesn't have any trees," Delma said, pointing toward the ground.

"Excellent, Delma," Bryn said. "You're so smart! I knew we brought you along for a reason."

"But if you had just looked right there, you would have seen it," Delma said. "That's not smart; even Crazy Gréog could have spotted that."

"It's still smart, though," Bryn said. "I know many people who are too dense to see three feet in front of them."

I'm landing now, Xolt said. *Stop arguing and hold on so I don't drop either of you!*

The landing was a bit rough; Xolt stumbled a few times before he regained his balance. Bryn was rather glad that his Bond did not fall over completely, for he did not want to be a crushed Bryn.

Sorry guys, Xolt said after he placed them on the ground. *I'm just tired.*

"You can say that again," Delma said.

Sorry guys, I'm just tired?

"He is tired," Delma said. "He's making silly jokes."

"And that differs from normal Xolt how?" Bryn asked.

Shut up and go kiss another tree, Xolt said.

"No, don't," Delma said. "The trees here are too pretty."

Bryn turned and took a closer look at the trees. The blue parts of the tree they had seen from the air were large flowers. The bark of the tree was a very dark shade of blue; Bryn had to blink a few times to be certain that he was not looking at a tree with black bark and blue flowers. They looked nothing like any trees he had seen before, but they were beautiful in their own way. They were as beautiful as a tree could be without being under the influence of mushrooms, anyway.

"Blueflower trees!" Delma exclaimed before she started running toward the grove.

"Blueflower trees?" Bryn asked. "That name certainly is…creative."

Right, Xolt said as he closed his eyes and let himself fall down a few feet away from Bryn. *You watch the girl. I'm going to rest.*

"Very well," Bryn said. "It's not like she can get into much trouble here."

"Mister Bryn! I've found a new friend!"

"What in the stars," Bryn groaned as he ran toward where it sounded like Delma's voice was coming from. Couldn't the girl go one day without some sort of chaos following close behind?

Delma appeared from behind one of the trees, carrying something tiny and white in her arms. As she got closer to Bryn, it began to squirm, revealing a head with two disproportionately large ears, beady eyes, and a tiny nose. Its tail spike nearly hit Delma, but it restrained itself at the last minute. It was not struggling to get away from her, like most sane creatures would do in the presence of small children; it was simply trying to get a better look at Bryn.

"Isn't she pretty? She said she was my friend," Delma said as she sat down on the grass.

"Oh no," Bryn said as he got a better look at the creature. "An Onizac?"

"I don't know what that is," Delma said.

"You're holding one," Bryn said. "Since she's a baby, she's probably Bonded to you. We'll have to carry her for the rest of the journey, and feed her, and deal with her possibly getting in the way."

The Onizac emitted several loud and high-pitched squeaks, causing Bryn to hold his hands to his head in pain.

"She says she is my Bond," Delma said. "And she doesn't like you very much."

"The feeling is mutual." Bryn said. "Onizacs are rather annoying."

What's this about Onizacs? Xolt asked, sounding quite grumpy. *If that's what's keeping me awake, tell it to be quiet.*

"She's not an it, she's a girl!" Delma exclaimed.

Fine. Does the girl have a name? Xolt asked.

"Not yet," Delma said. "I need to think of one."

Give her a name based on her attributes.

"Attributes?"

What she's like.

"Well, she's white, small, and she annoys Bryn," Delma said, pausing in thought for a moment. Then, she began to smile as if a brilliant idea had come to her. "I think I'll name her Mushroom."

"Mushroom!" Bryn exclaimed. "Shouldn't you give her a nice name like…err…Snowy? Snowball?"

"Those are silly names," Delma said. "I like Mushroom."

The Onizac kitten started purring as she curled up in Delma's lap.

"See, she likes the name, and she likes me!"

Bryn sighed. "Okay, so her name is Mushroom."

I told you coming here was a bad idea, Xolt said. *Now Delma is going to have to live up to some crazy prophecy.*

"Crazy prophecy?" Delma asked. "What did Mushroom do?"

She Bonded you, Xolt said. *Pretty soon, you'll start hearing her talk all the time. Then the fun begins; everyone will start coming to you, wondering when she's going to have kittens for them to Bond.*

And believe me, there will be plenty who will want Onizac kittens.

"Of course," Delma said. "Mushroom is pretty, and they'll all want pretty kitties."

"Yes, but having a pretty kitty means you'll Bond an Onizard," Bryn said. "At least, that's what Bral says."

"Bral?"

My dad, Xolt explained. *The story goes that the first ruler of the Sandleyr, Senbralni, found an Onizac kitten and liked it so much, that he brought as many as he could find back to the Sandleyr. He only gave them to Onizards he liked, so it was important to have one. Legend has it that when he died, some of his light went to those Onizards with the Onizac kittens, and when new Onizards were born, they became Bonds of the Onizards with the Onizac kittens. Ever since then, having an Onizac has been a guarantee that you'll Bond an Onizard.*

"That's silly!" Delma exclaimed. "Mushroom is my new friend, not some weird legend."

"Well, the truth is, Jena has an Onizac, and she's a Bond," Bryn said. "I don't have one, and I'm a Bond. To me they're nothing more than nuisance pets that survive on crazy prophecies."

"Well I'm keeping her, and that's final!" Delma said.

Fine, Xolt said. *You guys can both argue over the little Onizac when morning comes. It's getting too late for this nonsense.*

Bryn sighed as he looked and noticed the sun setting over the Blueflower trees. "Yes, let's get some rest. I have a feeling that tomorrow will be a long day."

Xolt sat down and closed his eyes, and Delma leaned on his shoulder, but Bryn could not go to sleep. Instead he watched the blue flowers on the trees slowly fade to black blurs as the light diminished around them.

Chapter 34

Enjoy this night, heir of Senbralni, the Fire Queen said. *It will be your last.*

Idenno shook his head, wondering how she thought her pathetic threats were going to affect him. It certainly didn't make him afraid of what was to come; it only proved that the Fire Queen was making herself more pathetic in her desperate attempts to make him despair. *How am I supposed to enjoy a night in which I am being watched by the most horrid demon who ever lived?*

You would not think me so horrid, if you were not so stubborn in your refusal to admit the truth.

Your truth, not mine, Idenno said. *Besides, tonight will not be my last. The Zarder is coming, and he will rescue us all.*

You must be losing a lot of blood, the Fire Queen said. *Now you're getting the Zarder's gender confused.*

My mistake, Idenno said, inwardly cursing himself. He didn't want Bryn to lose that element of surprise when he and Xoltorble finally arrived. The look of shock on the Fire Queen's face was going to be incredibly amusing when the time came; Idenno did not want to spoil that.

And you're smiling at your mistakes, the Fire Queen added. *I should call Ransenna, but I won't.*

How touching, Idenno said.

Indeed. I am wondering how I shall touch you next. I am too tired to enjoy myself, and I must save my energy. But at the same time, I want to destroy that pathetic grin of yours before it spreads like the disease it is.

I'm sorry, Idenno said. *You're stuck in a problem you cannot solve.*

Oh, believe me, I'll find a way, the Fire Queen said. *I have as much time as I need; you only have what time I give to you.*

What time you give to me is already decided, Idenno said. *The Great Lord of the Sky knows when I will die, and when I do, I will not give you the benefit of dying in pain. I have already felt the greatest pain possible; you cannot add to it, just as I cannot detract from it.*

Sky Lord, the Fire Queen said. *What pathetic nonsense. Your mother actually saw the one she claimed to love killed in front of her. You have only had to deal with rejection. I could kill everyone you believe that you love in front of you, and you would feel much greater pain from that. You can live through rejection; you cannot live through the deaths of those you believe you love.*

And I suppose you'd be the greatest expert in that field, Idenno said, *considering you can claim everyone you lust after without their permission. How many young boys and male non-natures have you claimed for your sick moments of pleasure? How many random deaths in the Sandleyr are your fault?*

Probably all of them, the Fire Queen said. *But I have not, nor will I ever claim young boys or male non-natures. Some things they say I've done are greatly exaggerated.* She smiled and closed her eyes for a while, as if imagining the acts she had committed in great detail. *If you'd like your ego inflated, I must admit that claiming you was one of my greatest of triumphs.*

You may have claimed my body, but you have never claimed me, Idenno said.

And that is why it was so deliciously pleasurable, the Fire Queen said, stepping closer to him and smiling as she looked at his body. *The proud and noble Watchzard pining away day after day, believing himself to be madly in love with Lady Rulsaesan. He saves every part of himself, and he trains and tones his body to utter perfection. He is so distant, so idealized by all, and yet in the end, he is merely an Onizard man. A handsome, conquerable man who struggled valiantly for his honor, and in failing raged against the injustice committed against him. I must say, Rulsaesan has no idea what she gave up when she chose Deyraeno over you.*

Idenno shuddered in disgust and terror. He could not decide if this ridiculous new emotional torment was worse than the physical pain he was suffering, but it was definitely utterly creepy. *Have you no soul? Do you not have any care for the others whatsoever?*

Of course not, the Fire Queen said. *The world is my enemy, and so I can destroy it and mold it to my will. But it does not have to be that way, Idenno; I will spare you, if you make the choice that pleases me.*

What? Idenno asked. He was utterly mortified by the very idea of things that pleased the Fire Queen.

It does not have to end in your death; if you simply give up your lust for Rulsaesan, and pledge your loyalty to me, I will tell Ransenna to heal you, and I will treat you with all the respect you deserve. Perhaps I can help you finally enjoy that which you despise; I am certain that I am not as ugly in appearance as you claim I am out of spite. Believing in Rulsaesan has made you blind to all else; let me help you see.

Never, Idenno said. *Do you think I would be here now if giving up my love were so easy? Even if your offer was not a lie, I would not accept it. An honorable death is better than a terrible life as your pleasure slave.*

Pleasure slave? the Fire Queen asked as she laughed. *You are such a prude.*

You disgusting demon, Idenno said. *I'd rather be a prude than a callous murderer.*

So you've said many times, the Fire Queen said. *Absolutely perfect and moral, even as he knows he will die. It is an amazing trait that my enemies seem to have. If I knew where you got it from, I would claim that power for myself and use it against you.*

I am moral because I know it helps those I love, Idenno said. *As long as you doubt love's existence, you will never have that power.*

I may never have that power, the Fire Queen said, *but I do not need it. You seem to suffer greatly from it, while I simply enjoy myself as I please, and I am happy. But it seems there is no way to convince you that I have chosen the better path.*

Why did you just try to convince me to be like you, then? Idenno asked. *Why try to destroy love when you don't even believe it exists?*

Because I like to see my enemies suffer before they die. But it seems your foolish belief in loyalty and love has made you suffer enough all on your own. Now what is left is to torment those two fools you think you have been protecting.

Chapter 35

Ransenna paced back and forth, worrying about what was to come. The week had slowly slipped away, and now both she and Deldenno were in grave danger. How was she going to fight back if the Zarder didn't come? It certainly didn't seem like she was coming. At most, the Fire Queen had a day's head start; if this was the case, the Zarder should have been arrived by now.

Are you okay, Ranse? Deldenno asked, frowning as he watched her. *You seem upset.*

I'm just worried, that's all, Ransenna said. *I'm sorry if I've worried you as well.*

There's no need to apologize, Ranse, Deldenno said. *We're all worried right now. But the Zarder will come; I am certain of it.*

I am glad that you are no longer depressed, Delden, Ransenna said. *I was worried about you.*

You should be worried about yourself, the Fire Queen said. *Ransenna! I need you to heal Idenno.*

Ransenna sighed. *Yes, Fire Queen,* she said as she walked away from Delden. She didn't want to leave him alone, but if the Fire Queen had determined Idenno needed healing, he had to be in bad shape.

I find it amusing that you've started calling him by a nickname, the Fire Queen said. *Though I doubt you have told him the secret you were supposed to have told him.*

What good would that do? Ransenna asked. *He doesn't need to know that secret. My past is behind me; I am no longer your servant, and I am no longer bound to past mistakes.*

Ah, but I believe he does need to know, the Fire Queen said. *Imagine what would happen if your dear Delden learned that you lusted after another.*

I once loved another, Ransenna said. *That is true. But that is behind me; I have no feelings for him anymore.*

Love? The Fire Queen sneered. *You fool. You should have learned by now that love does not exist. You may have had some sort of compassion for him that was mixed with your lust, but it was not love. If Delden died today, you would not mourn his death.*

You have no right to tell me what I would or would not do, Ransenna said. *If you planned to kill him today, you'd have to kill me first.*

Such compassion and lack of care for your own life, the Fire Queen said, shaking her head as she started to laugh. *I seem to remember this annoying trait from another Onizard. Her name was Isenna, and she was just as foolish as you.*

You liar, Ransenna snapped as she trembled from holding back her rage. *You know nothing of my mother. She was a hero of the Sandleyr for her sacrifice.*

A hero? The Sandleyr has always been quick to give that title to those who do not deserve it. the Fire Queen said. *I was there to see her so-called sacrifice, and it was not as glorious as you seem to believe it was.*

What are you talking about? How is that even possible?

Didn't you ever consider the gaps in that story about your mother? The Fire Queen asked. *How could you possibly believe she simply died from healing, even if she was healing someone as hopeless as Leyrkan Mekanni? Children of Earth are built for healing; it is their sole purpose in life. Why would fulfilling her purpose in life kill her?*

Children of Earth can still die if they overextend themselves.

Indeed, and Isenna did overextend herself. She tried to heal the new Leyrkan, Mekanni, when he was sick.

Sick? Ransenna asked.

Surely everyone in the Sandleyr has heard of that nonsense by now, the Fire Queen said. *I dare say it was my greatest triumph, creating an imaginary illness in an Onizard who once thought himself so powerful and indestructible. Now he is weak, and every time that he remembers the night I forced him to cheat on his precious Delsenni, he becomes a sniveling coward who dwells in the past.*

What does that have to do with my mother trying to heal him? Ransenna asked. *I see nothing in that other than further proof that you are a demon.*

Oh, I know I am a demon, the Fire Queen said. *That's no secret now. But it was when I first became the Fire Queen. When I ruled the Sandleyr, no one could question my absolute authority. Those who did became pathetic Watchzards or incinerated carcasses at my disposal. But that depended on no one knowing the secret of how I gained my power. Your mother was a witness to the Leyrque of Night's death under my claws!*

How? Ransenna asked as she started to cry. *That's not possible; she was asleep, or taking care of me.*

Children of Light have the power to show memories, the Fire Queen said. *I know this; my mother was a Child of Light, before I killed her. Mekanni lost his ability to control that power when he was sick, and your mother saw something she should not have seen. She confronted me, the fool.*

You killed her, Ransenna whispered.

Of course I killed her! the Fire Queen. *She was threatening to tell the entire Sandleyr the truth! I would have lost my title, my dignity, and my power. She was already half-insane, so who would have believed her death was anything other than an accident? She died rather quickly, if that makes you feel any better.*

You speak of this as if it's a simple thing, Ransenna said slowly as her tail swayed involuntarily. *How could you kill an innocent Onizard who only wanted to do what was right?*

She was no innocent who was slaughtered without warning. She had her chance to conceal what she had learned from Mekanni. But she made a stupid choice, and paid for it with her life. She knew, as soon as she confronted me, that she would die. She even said so as she threatened to tell the whole Sandleyr. But she still confronted me. Call her a hero for that if you wish, but do not worship her for anything less than the truth of what she was. She was just a simple Child of Earth who learned too much and paid for it, not a saintly healer who overextended herself.

Why did you convince me to work for you, knowing I was the daughter of your enemy? Ransenna asked.

If I recall correctly, you worked for me willingly, the Fire Queen said.

You promised me that you would introduce me to my first love, Ransenna said, *and you told me foolish lies that I believed without question.*

Oh please, the Fire Queen said. *Stop calling him your first love and call him by his name. I promised to introduce you to Delbralfi, and I did. You both got along very well indeed, until you didn't follow my advice to give in to your lusts.*

I could not do those unspeakable things to him, Ransenna said, shuddering at the memory. *You wanted me to...to rape him! I loved him, and you were telling me to just use him as an object.*

Men are nothing but objects, The Fire Queen said. *They will try to treat you like you are an object, but in reality, they are the ones who are so easy to manipulate. They are the ones who desperately try to hide themselves from the truth of life that all must come to realize; men are useless for anything other than the pleasure of females or the continuation of the species. I was only trying to help you see the truth. But you rejected it for the falsehood of love and supposed equality between you and Delbralfi. I must say, it was most amusing to learn that he didn't even have the same lusts for you.*

You demon, Ransenna said as she wept uncontrollably. *And you told him that I shared your views. He said he heard a rumor, and didn't believe me until many years later, after your terrible reign was finally ended. In fact, I think he still only pretends to believe me. Our friendship ended because of you!*

At least he gained the wisdom not to trust in rumors, and you were freed from the pain of believing in love.

No I was not, Ransenna said. *I was just in even more pain. Of course, you enjoyed that, for it just made me frustrated enough to believe you when you said that humans were nothing but animals. When I think of the sins I committed, I-*

You did not know, the Fire Queen. *You cannot sin if you do not know you are sinning. Besides, killing humans is not a sin.*

Yes it is, Ransenna said. *I was wrong to kill, for I dishonored the Code of Earth, the Sandleyr, and myself. I should have turned myself in to Mekanni then and become a non-nature for my crimes. But I blindly believed you, even when I knew that you had been wrong before. If I had not met the Zarder, I would have still been blindly following the path you created for me, being your mindless little protégé for the rest of my life. But I am not your mindless little protégé anymore; I am Ransenna, daughter of Isenna, and if I have to meet my mother's fate for resisting you, I will.*

Very well, the Fire Queen said. *I should kill you now, but I'd much rather kill you when you don't believe you are dying a martyr's death. Just know that you could die at any moment from this point on.*

That is no different from before, Ransenna said, but inwardly she became afraid. Would the Fire Queen kill her before she told Deldenno the truth about her feelings? Or, worse, would she kill Ransenna after she had told Deldenno the truth, at the very moment when she saw the hurt in his eyes and knew that he did not return those feelings?

What is different is the order of the deaths, the Fire Queen said. *I had planned to be merciful to you, but you will not see reason. Your precious Deldenno will be the first to die.*

No, cried Ransenna. *Please, spare him.*

Oh, I won't kill him right now, the Fire Queen laughed. *But I believe it is time that I talk to him. If you want him to live a while longer, do not go near him until I am through.*

Chapter 36

Deldenno waited patiently for Ransenna to return. She had been gone for far too long for his comfort, and the week was almost gone. He had no doubts that the Fire Queen could and would kill earlier than her appointed time.

Delden shuddered and desperately prayed to the Lord of the Sky that Ransenna was still alive. He wanted to tell her that he loved her; he had missed many opportunities out of fear, and he did not want all opportunities to be lost forever. Furthermore, if Ransenna was dead, then so was Idenno, and Deldenno was surely next.

I need to stop worrying, Delden said to himself. Idenno had told him the Fire Queen liked to be manipulative; she was probably keeping Ranse away somehow, knowing how losing her would affect him.

Indeed, the Fire Queen said as she walked toward him. *Your death will come when it is your turn. In the meantime, I would like to talk to you.*

I would not like to talk to you, Delden said, turning his head away.

I think you would, the Fire Queen said as she grabbed his leg again.

Delden winced. *What do you want, demon?*

181

I want you to talk reason into Watchzard Idenno, the Fire Queen said. *He's delusional; he thinks that he's protecting you and your mother by resisting me and Ransenna.*

Talk reason into him? Delden asked. *What do you mean, resist you and Ransenna? Ransenna is not on your side.*

How do you know? The Fire Queen asked. *Have you seen her every time she went away from you? Have you watched her every move, noted her every emotion, and questioned her every action? She could have easily flown both you and herself away, if she truly wanted to escape.*

I asked her to stay, Deldenno said. *You would have killed Idenno if we had fled.*

My only hostage? The Fire Queen asked. *I think not. That is just Ransenna's excuse. She was always good at concocting the best lies and getting others to believe them.*

An amusing thought, coming from you. You are the queen of lies and deception; you nearly destroyed many lives through your selfish ambition, including Ransenna's life.

Ransenna still works for me, the Fire Queen explained. *I asked her to tell you from the start; I didn't want poor Deldenno, son of Rulsaesan to get in over his head. I asked her to work for me, because I knew she was the only Child of Earth I could trust to do my bidding. Did you not consider there may have been a reason she was so kind, so concerned about you? It was all an act for me.*

You liar, Delden said as he shuddered. He had to believe it wasn't true. The alternative was too horrible to contemplate.

How can you know? The Fire Queen asked. *How can you tell that she is not just using you to get information for me? I can tell you for a fact that every time she comes to me, she discusses your actions in great detail, and I study them to learn your weaknesses.*

Deldenno frowned, thinking back on all the times Ransenna had said she was leaving to heal Idenno. He tried to remember her reactions, wondering if there was some hidden meaning in them. Could Ransenna truly be a traitor?

No, she could not. Deldenno's mind drifted to that cold night when she so willingly, so kindly kept him warm. Remembering the look of joy in her eyes as he smiled at him, he knew that Ransenna could not have possibly meant anything foul; the Fire Queen's lies would try to show Ransenna in a negative light, but Deldenno could not see her as anything other than the most wonderful Onizard in the world.

You did well, Deldenno said. *That almost sounded like the truth. But I trust Ransenna; she has never left my side throughout this ordeal, except in times of Idenno's greatest need.*

The foolish Watchzard has been needy, the Fire Queen said. *He moans and complains about every little wound I've given anyone, and then he sings praises of Leyrque Rulsaesan.*

Everyone sings praises of my mother, Deldenno said. *She is a good Leyrque.*

Not everyone lusts after her the way Idenno does, the Fire Queen said.

What? Deldenno exclaimed.

You didn't know? You truly are a fool; your mother is all he thinks about all day long. He lives and breathes her, and cries whenever he thinks of how he will never have his precious Rulsaesan. He probably only tolerates you because of your connection to your mother. You do look so much like her.

What are you implying? Deldenno asked.

His mother was a lesbian, you know. Then again, she did end up becoming the joinmate of a man later in life. I suppose Idenno may have inherited the ability to be flexible in his lusts; and you do look so much like your mother. The resemblance is incredible.

You monster! Deldenno screamed. *Calling you a demon is an insult to the lowest of demons. Idenno is like a second father to me; he is not like that at all! Just because you are controlled by your lusts does not mean that everyone in the world is controlled by lusts! Idenno is a good, innocent Onizard; I will not have you claim those nasty things about him.*

Innocent? The Fire Queen started laughing hysterically, carrying on for a minute before she said, *Idenno is hardly innocent. He argued with his own grandfather for months, forsaking his title as heir of the Night Kingdom just for the sake of his lust for Rulsaesan. He could have had a good joinmate of a noble bloodline and children of his own, but instead he chose to be a surrogate father to whelps like you. He could have been a much better Leyrkan than Mekanni, but instead he chose to be an insignificant Watchzard after I threatened death to Rulsaesan if he didn't take that job.*

How does any of that make him awful? Deldenno asked. *It seems to me that if he loved my mother, then he should not have become the joinmate of another. It's just common decency, something you seem to lack. I know that I would take the job of Watchzard if it meant protecting those I love. If Idenno truly does love my mother, then I see nothing wrong with that. My mother constantly talks of what a good and noble friend he is; if she could sense any malice in him towards me, she would not say those things.*

She is afraid of him, the Fire Queen said. *He is so much stronger than she is, and if she upsets him, he can overpower her. Frankly, I'm surprised that he hasn't already.*

It was Deldenno's turn to laugh hysterically. *Your lies are getting even more pathetic. Idenno, the skinny former Watchzard, overpowering my mother, the powerful Child of Light with a tall, strong husband capable of winning any fight he gets himself into? The idea is utterly ludicrous. Your warped view of the world does not affect me, for I know that it is just that; a warped, twisted untruth.*

The Fire Queen rolled her eyes. *I see that there is no convincing you of the truth. A pity; my enemies should always die knowledgeable of their terrible mistakes. But it doesn't matter; you have just convinced me who I ought to kill first. Ransenna begged me to kill you first, for she wanted to end your suffering. But I will kill Idenno, then Ransenna, then you.*

First you will have to kill the Zarder, Deldenno said, *and I don't think you can.*

Chapter 37

It was midday; Zarder Bryn and Xolt stood in a small trail of short grass that lead to the field of tall grass. They were waiting for Delma to return from her scouting mission. The girl was more useful than she could have given herself credit for; it was hard to hear her moving along the edge of the woods. There were times when Bryn could vaguely see a green shape moving about, but those were few and far between. Delma could learn much more than he could this way, and they wouldn't lose the element of surprise, even with the annoying little Onizac following her around.

"Mister Bryn," the girl whispered. "Is it safe for me to come back now?"

"Yes," Bryn whispered. "What happened? What did you see?"

"There are three Onizards there, and the dragon is bossing them around. For some reason, two of them are close together and separated from the dragon and the other Onizard."

"What colors were they?"

"The two Onizards close together are dark green and dark blue, and the Onizard near the dragon is a lighter shade of blue."

Idenno, Xolt said. *Why would she be keeping Idenno separate from the others?*

Bryn frowned. "I can think of a few reasons, but I don't want to find out if I'm right."

"What are we going to do, Mister Bryn?" Delma asked.

"What you are going to do is stay put," Bryn said. "Xolt and I don't need you getting in the way of the dragon's breath."

"But I can help!" Delma exclaimed. "Tell me how I can help!"

Try scouting the rest of the tall grass without being seen, Xolt said. *Then, when you see the dragon fly away, or I call you back, come meet us by the other Onizards. We need to make sure the dragon hasn't hidden anything that could change the way this battle will go.*

"Okay," Delma said as she ran and disappeared into the tall grass. There was not much to be seen of her anymore, other than the strange way the grass moved as she went through it. Mushroom the Onizac blinked a few times, then ran into the tall grass after her, squeaking as if in protest of her abandonment.

"That will take forever," Bryn observed.

I know, Xolt said as he grinned. *But she feels like she's doing something important, and she's out of harm's way.*

"Unless the Fire Queen torches her area of the tall grass," Bryn said.

She won't, Xolt said. *Delma has a good sense of direction; she won't be stupid enough to go near what she calls the dragon. Now we just need to plan what we're going to do.*

"We shouldn't rush in there," Bryn said. "We need to wait until the Fire Queen is distracted somehow."

Distracted how? As in trying to kill someone distracted, or some other form of distracted?

"We'll take whatever we can get," Bryn said. "We just need to make sure it's not 'I just killed someone and now I'm oblivious' distracted."

She's not going to kill anyone, Xolt said. *Not if I have anything to do with it. Let's go, Bryn; I am ready.*

Chapter 38

Idenno listened carefully to the sounds that came from the woods. It sounded as if something was attempting to move about quietly. It was eerie hearing such noise coming from the wood when it had been silent in the days he had spent waiting for the Zarder and his Bond. Were they arriving now? If so, they had certainly lost the element of surprise.

There are often groups of strange creatures who roam near here, the Fire Queen said as she walked toward him. *They are taller than humans, but they are still much shorter than even the smallest of Onizards. They run on four legs, and have long snouts. They have no tails that I can see, but they have long hair where a tail should be, and this same hair also grows on their necks. They only have one horn, and that is no defense for a strong Onizard like me. I thought I had gotten rid of them all, but apparently not.*

Why must you kill everything? Idenno asked, closing his eyes in sadness.

Why shouldn't I kill everything that is disagreeable to me? the Fire Queen asked. *If I can destroy what vexes me, why should I not do it?*

Kill me then, and let Deldenno and Ransenna return to the Sandleyr and stop vexing you.

Ah, but I cannot do that now, the Fire Queen said. *Senraeno is coming; I don't want him to go back. I want my revenge.*

Revenge is useless, Idenno said. *It cannot destroy the real problem you have with the world. Why go on this futile quest to harm others, when you can just set your problems aside?*

I'm sorry, I forgot noble Idenno's view of the world. The only way to destroy your problems is to run away from them, like you ran away from your kingdom and your family.

Idenno scowled. *I had to leave the Night Kingdom. I was not going to make the same mistake my mother did and compromise my true love for the sake of producing heirs of Senbralni. My grandfather was going to have me joinmated to some random Onizard who didn't deserve the pain of knowing she wasn't loved.*

Random? the Fire Queen said quietly. *I think not. That Onizard was me.*

You? Idenno's eyes widened, and for once he had nothing to shout back at her.

What, you are shocked that I was capable of proving my worth to Mesenni? My father was of much more noble blood than my worthless, good-for-nothing mother. He had persuaded Mesenni to let me become your joinmate and continue the line of Senbralni.

The Fire Queen began to tremble. *When you left the Night Kingdom, I was essentially a useless Onizard. All my adult life I had been prepared to be a noble lady, and for what? I could not even attract young Mekanno; when he became Mekanni, he joinmated Delsenfi and I learned the truth. Once a Child of Light has blessed a union, it does not matter if both parties are interested or not; they cannot joinmate another.*

Was being a joinmate what you really wanted? Idenno asked as he suddenly felt sick to his stomach and furious at a dead Onizard at the same time.

The Fire Queen stood completely still, betraying no emotion. *My father was so disgraced by your rejection that he threw himself off the Sandleyr wall into the sea. He was finally gaining hope again after my mother left him, and you killed that hope. It is your fault I am utterly alone in this world,* The Fire Queen said, turning her glare once more onto Idenno. But this time it was not a glare of blind hatred she gave everyone; it was the cool and calculating glare reserved only for the greatest of enemies.

You would have been just as alone in the world if I had agreed to become your joinmate, Idenno said. *How much more disgrace would fall on your father if I had heartlessly agreed and damned you to a life of suffering as I ignored you for Rulsaena who would become Rulsaesan?*

The Fire Queen laughed for a long time before she responded. *Oh, do not make the mistake of thinking this is all some silly plot to avenge myself of the shame and disgrace I suffered for you. It is not; I want nothing to do with you now, save perhaps as a toy to throw around and damage as I may. The thought of anything else disgusts me.*

Then why do you act as if there is something to avenge? Idenno asked. *If I broke your heart, I am sorry, but there is nothing I can do. No amount of destroying me will help you get your father back.*

How dare you! the Fire Queen screamed, slamming her tail against his side repeatedly. *I may have lusted after you at one point, but that is utterly through. Besides, that was no reason to joinmate you! I wanted the power that came from being able to manipulate the heir of Senbralni, not some socially acceptable way to use my lusts! My heart was never broken! It still pumps blood through my body, and I will be able to put you in your place again for such foolish talk! You have no authority, no right to tell me I cannot get my father back! It is no wonder Rulsaesan was uninterested in you, you pathetic, hideous fool! You are right in thinking you are not Senbralni's heir, for no sane ruler would choose someone as repulsive as you as their heir!*

Idenno at first tried to struggle back against the blows, but he soon realized it was pointless. His whole body ached, and his breath came in short, quick gasps. He tried to control his breathing, to maintain some level of composure in the madness. But he found that it was all in vain, and slowly gave in to the overwhelming pain.

The Fire Queen stopped her barrage of painful blows, stared at him for a moment, then screamed, *Ransenna! I'm losing him!*

Idenno was vaguely aware of the Child of Earth approaching and talking to him, but he could not understand what she was saying. He'd get better? Everything would be fine soon? That didn't make sense; he was in the land of the demons. He could hear her voice attempting to calm him, but it did not truly register until he felt the cool touch of her healing powers at work. Then there was nothing but more pain, the fear in Ransenna's eyes, and the hatred of the Fire Queen.

You are dismissed for now. Go tend to that other pathetic whelp, she said to Ransenna, who promptly obeyed. Then the Fire Queen spun around to face Idenno and said, *Next time, I will let you die. Never speak of my father again.*

Then never speak of Rulsaesan again, Idenno said. *Such a fair Onizard does not deserve to be in your thoughts.*

I could say the same thing about my father and your thoughts, The Fire Queen said. *You are lucky that I am tired from the journey; I would have continued to beat you for a considerably longer time if I could have gotten away with it.*

Lucky me, Idenno said as he drifted off to sleep despite his best efforts to stay awake. His last thought was to wonder if Deldenno and Ransenna would be able to handle the wrath of the Fire Queen.

Chapter 39

Ransenna returned to Deldenno, shivering in fear in spite of her best efforts. Up until this point, she had managed to fool Delden into believing that she was in control of the situation. But now she was losing hope. If the Fire Queen was beating Idenno to the point of sending him into shock, it was only a matter of time before she and Deldenno were threatened.

What happened, Ranse? What is wrong? Delden asked. *You look like you've seen a ghost.*

Idenno...she hurt him, Ransenna said as she started to cry. *She hurt him much worse than she has before. He's suffering, and my powers are useless. We are all going to die out here, one by one.*

Don't start talking like that, Delden said in a commanding but comforting tone. *You brought me out of my depression, so you cannot sink into a depression of your own. Iden is still alive, isn't he?*

Of course; the Fire Queen needs her hostages alive.

Then you have done some good, Ranse, the Child of Water said. *You've kept us all alive, and you've given us hope when all hope seemed to be lost. Don't you dare start losing hope, or I'll have to give up as well. I don't want to do that; I want to live to see…happier times for us all.*

Happier times? Ransenna asked as she looked into his eyes. If she were a Child of Light, she might have been overwhelmed by the courage and gentleness contained within those grey eyes; even though she was a mere Child of Earth, she was taken aback. Looking at those eyes and the smile that went with them, she could almost forget the pain and destruction around her. She could almost believe that the happier times truly would come.

Yes, happier times, Delden said.

There was trust in his voice, and Ransenna realized that she trusted him more than any other Onizard. She trusted him even more than she had trusted her first love before he rejected her so coldly. It was now that she had to tell him the truth; no other time would come. She wanted him to know, but at the same time, she feared losing the trust he had given her. After she had taken a deep breath, Ransenna said, *Delden, there's something I need to tell you.*

Really? he asked as he tilted his head slightly and blinked in puzzlement.

Yes, came the voice of the Fire Queen as she appeared from behind Ransenna. *She most definitely has something to tell you. I think I will be the one who tells you, though. You'll find it rather interesting, I think.*

No, Ransenna said as she began to cry. *Please don't…*

Before you were born, Miss Ransenna fell in love with your Bond. Her true love was Delbralfi.

No, Ransenna repeated softly, fearing to even look at Deldenno.

195

Or, at least, she lusted after him. Rumor has it she even tried to use him as an object of her pleasure.

That was a rumor started by you! Ransenna screamed.

Of course it was, the Fire Queen said, rolling her eyes as if Ransenna was just a silly fool who would not admit the truth. *It was most amusing seeing you sob your little heart out over the pathetic whelp of Mekanni. But it did not last for long; you got over your pathetic desires and moved on with your life of service to me, killing humans when I ordered you to kill them. I saved you from a great amount of pain. I doubt, however, that you'll find time to thank me.*

I moved on, Ransenna said, *but it took years of pain from believing that I was worthless and good for nothing but preventing the inevitable deaths of Onizards for a little while. I learned in time that I was worthwhile and got over the rejection and humiliation. But it was a struggle that I almost did not win. However, for one tiny bit of nothing I can thank you; I did learn to be myself.*

You loved Delbralfi, and you killed humans? Deldenno asked. Out of the corner of her eye, Ransenna thought she caught him hanging his head in shame.

I did, she admitted. *But that was a long time ago, before Zarder Jena saved my life, when I was young and stupid.*

You admit your stupidity in believing that love exists, then? The Fire Queen asked as she grinned.

Ransenna could see that the Fire Queen was delighting in the idea of a world without love, and it angered her greatly. *No, I do not. I admit that*

Delbralfi was not the right Onizard for me, but I do not admit that I was stupid to love him. If love is stupid, then the world is not worth living in. There is one important fact you seem to have overlooked, Fire Queen: I have no feelings for Delbralfi anymore, but that is because I have found a more worthy love. At this she finally forced herself to look at Delden and whisper, *I found you, Delden.*

Deldenno, son of Rulsaesan? The Fire Queen laughed as she stared at Ransenna. *You have certainly moved down and acquired even more pathetic lusts.*

Deldenno frowned as he looked at Ransenna, as if he were trying to figure out the right words to say.

Ransenna smiled meekly back at him until she could not take it anymore. It was too much; she didn't want to look at him as he rejected her. She turned toward the Fire Queen, raised her head proudly, and said, *You certainly know much about lusts, Fire Queen. Perhaps because you care so much about yourself, lusts are all you are capable of having. You may think that I am weak for caring about someone other than myself, but I see it as my greatest strength. It proves that I have a soul that is still worthy of a star. I love Deldenno, son of Rulsaesan, and now that he knows, I am not afraid to say it anymore. If those words damn me to an early death, then death is unavoidable.*

You would die for an Onizard man like Deldenno, when he doesn't even share the same feelings as you? The Fire Queen shook her head. *You are more pathetic than I originally thought, Ransenna. Clearly owing your life to a human has made you weak.*

She is not pathetic, Deldenno said as he lifted his head off the ground. *Do not try to tell me what my feelings are, foul demon of fire. I love Ransenna, too, and I would die for her just as quickly as she would die for me.*

You do? Ransenna asked incredulously as she whipped her head around. She would have smiled for joy if it had not been such a grim situation.

I do, Deldenno said calmly as he looked into her eyes.

I-I am sorry I didn't tell you before, Ransenna said as she resisted the urge to cry tears of joy mixed with sorrow.

Don't be, Deldenno said as he grasped her tail with his. *I am just glad we could tell each other before it was too late.*

It is certainly too late for your everlasting happiness, the Fire Queen said as she calmly stepped closer to the other Onizards. *I will laugh at your broken bodies, and you will die next to each other!* The Fire Queen screamed, lifting her tail to strike down Ransenna.

Ransenna saw the Fire Queen's tail start falling, but before she could react, a blur of grey rushed in front of her like a spring breeze bringing renewal. The blur of grey became a small grey Onizard who successfully blocked the Fire Queen's killer blow with his own tail.

No they won't, Xoltorble said. *They will laugh at the sight of your dead body.*

Chapter 40

Xolt stared into the crimson eyes of the Fire Queen, unwilling to look away. He had gained the element of surprise, but if he looked toward anything else, the Fire Queen would use his moment of distraction against him. Not even the hideous scar under her eye caught his attention for more than a second. Xolt could not afford to give the Fire Queen the advantage.

Green eyes, the knack for getting into other Onizards' business, and questionable abilities, the Fire Queen said c. *This hatchling must be the child of Teltrena the non-nature.*

Her name is Lady Teltresan of the Day Kingdom, Xolt said, *and I am not a hatchling.*

Very well, Hatchling. I asked specifically for Senraeno. Truly not even a hatchling would be stupid enough to confuse himself with Senraeno, the mighty hero of the Sandleyr.

Specific? I think not, Xolt said as he laughed. *You asked for the Zarder and the Zarder's Bond. How were we to know you meant Senraeno and Jena?*

I wanted my revenge on the human and Onizard who disgraced me! the Fire Queen shouted as she shook her head in frustration. *Not some hatchling and human who thought he or she was brave just because he is the Bond of a non-nature's child.*

"Well, I believe I have disgraced you in the past, and I'm sure if put to the test, Xolt can disgrace you today," Bryn said as he walked toward Ransenna and Deldenno.

Senme, The Fire Queen said. If she did not use telepathic speech, she would have spat the word.

"Indeed," Bryn said. "I'm sorry that I'm not sorry that Zarder Jena could not attend the party you've set up here. I hope that Zarder Senme and Xolt will suffice."

This just proves that the hatchling is a bigger fool than I originally suspected, the Fire Queen said. *You, a Bond! It's laughable.*

"It is rather funny, especially since your bad wording and my bad timing brought us here," Bryn said. "But enough of that. Xolt, I think you know what to do."

Out of the corner of his eye, Xolt saw Ransenna heal Deldenno's leg. Grinning, he moved his tail and hit the Fire Queen before dodging her first fire blast.

Bryn watched his Bond dance around the deadly flames as if it was a simple training exercise. He knew that Xolt was afraid; after all, Bryn was afraid too, and there was no shame in that. But Xolt was young, and he was strong, and he was swift; those flames were not destined to hit him.

Bryn tore his eyes away from the battle to find the Child of Earth. "Ransenna! I need you to heal the injured Onizards, then help us escape. There's a-"

Silence, Senme! The Fire Queen shouted as she set the grass around them on fire, trapping Bryn in the same general area as Ransenna and Deldenno. Idenno was separate and alone, though he was crawling closer to them for some inexplicable reason.

If I heal them both completely, I will use all of my strength, Ransenna said.

I will carry you, Deldenno said.

I'll kill you both, then, the Fire Queen said smugly. *As soon as I kill this pathetic hatchling and his even more pathetic human Bond.*

I meant what I said. I am willing to die for you, Ransenna, Deldenno said. Bryn could tell that he was on the verge of tears. *It is the only path fit for one who loves another.*

Ransenna, don't worry about me. Heal Delden completely when the time is right, Idenno said.

Ransenna blinked in surprise and confusion; so many had been speaking to her in an attempt to influence her decision. She had been paying so much attention to the problem in front of her and the fight between Xoltorble and the Fire Queen that she had almost forgotten about the former Watchzard. *What? Completely? What about you? You need it more than he does.*

Just do it, he snapped.

Ransenna shuddered. There was a disturbingly commanding tone to Idenno's voice. *Very well. How will I know when the time is right?*

You will, Idenno said, turning his head toward Xoltorble and the Fire Queen. *You will know well.*

Xoltorble attempted to speed past another fire blast, only to feel it hit his tail feathers. Wincing, he stopped to put out the fire in the dirt, only to discover a terrible dilemma: the Fire Queen had him cornered. If he moved again, her next blast would hit the three hostages and Bryn. If he did not move, the blast would hit him.

The Fire Queen saw this too, and she began to laugh. *Foolish Onizard. It's a pity you chose such a fool to be your Bond. Perhaps Senme will get his hope to be among the stars.*

"Perhaps Senme is getting tired of hearing you speak," Bryn said, though Xolt could tell he was just putting on a brave face. In his heart, both he and his Bond were afraid of the death that was surely coming.

Xolt looked back toward Bryn and the hostages. He did not want to see his death coming. Ransenna and Deldenno were watching him carefully and sadly, as if they were remembering the last stand of Xoltorble, the Child of Wind who tried to prevent their deaths. Erfasfi would live on to keep his memory, and perhaps Jena would name her child after his or her noble father. It was not so bad to die young and a hero.

The sound of the Fire Queen's flame breath hitting something filled the air, and Xolt felt no pain. Was this what it was like to die? But Xolt thought he would not be able to see any more once he died, and he was positive that Bryn would not be still standing, even if he did have an expression of mortified shock. Bryn, Ransenna, and Deldenno were all staring in horror at something behind him, and Idenno was...not where he had been before the fight began.

Idenno? Xolt asked, spinning around before he began to scream in terror at what he saw.

The Fire Queen was standing over Idenno's body. His wings were still unfurled from jumping in the way of the Fire Queen's blast, though there was not much left of them. Most of his body was badly burned, and his normally observant eyes were suddenly completely still, widened as if in a revelation of sudden and complete pain. His tail was twitching, but no other part of him was moving.

Idenno! Xolt shouted, desperately hoping for the best, hoping that the former Watchzard would show some form of life. Xolt could think of nothing but the story of how his mother was revived after nearly dying to save Senraeno. She became a Child of Light after that. Iden could become a Child of Light as well, couldn't he? Couldn't he get up again as if nothing was wrong in the first place? Couldn't he turn to his friends and say that everything was safe again?

No, he couldn't. That would be one of Bryn's stories, wouldn't it? The stories Bryn said could never come true, even when the world would be a better place if they did. Waiting for the nightmare to end would be acting like a child, and Xolt was not one. Not anymore. Now there was nothing but pain and tears.

Uncle Iden! Deldenno screamed, flying past Xolt with sudden vigor as he began to fight the Fire Queen. It was a swift victory, for the Fire Queen was suddenly in shock, as if this accidental death was far more terrible than her other deeds.

No! Someone tell him to get up! The Fire Queen screamed hysterically.

You demon! Don't you dare try to show sympathy now! Delden shouted, his eyes gleaming with hatred and tears. *You've killed him! You've killed the most innocent Onizard who ever lived. But that doesn't matter to you; he's just one more prize to add to your collection of kills.*

Father, don't leave me! The Fire Queen sobbed in a voice that was not entirely her own. *Don't leave me! Mother, how could you?* Then, after weakly parrying Delden's attacks, she took off as if the battle didn't matter to her anymore. Delden briefly debated flying after her, but then he simply gave up when he realized that doing so would negate Idenno's sacrifice. He turned back toward the body, but he could not look at it for long before he broke down and started crying uncontrollably.

Delden, a calm, comforting voice said.

Delden looked up to see the spirit of Idenno standing by the edge of the tall grass. Idenno was smiling, and his eyes were brown again. He seemed at peace, but Delden was still full of grief. *Uncle Iden, please don't go to the stars.*

I won't yet. I have things left to do, and a lady who needs me, Idenno said. *Take care of her.*

Of course I'll take care of my mother, Deldenno said.

No, take care of her, Idenno said, glancing in Ransenna's direction before turning toward the tall grass. *And her,* he added before his spirit began moving quickly away.

Iden, don't go! Deldenno screamed as he began to chase the spirit.

Delden! Ransenna shouted with a commanding tone that forced him to stop where he was. *Do not chase after him. All of the speed of wind could not catch him now.*

You are right as always, Ransenna, Deldenno said as he collapsed.

He was a white goose among the wild geese, Ransenna said as she walked to him and stood over him protectively, examining him for any new injuries. *I know what that means now.*

There had better be a good explanation for comparing the Onizard who saved our lives to a goose, Deldenno said, more harshly than he intended.

Idenno was a far greater Onizard than any of us; he stood out from everyone around him. He could have easily become an Onizard of great renown, but he chose to remain a simple Watchzard. He stayed with the wild geese like us, and he didn't choose that path just because it seemed funny, or because he didn't have a better path to choose. He chose that because of love. He loved you like you were his son, and he would not want you to suffer because of him.

He told me to take care of you, Delden said as he turned his head toward her, letting his skin absorb his tears.

Really? Ransenna smiled. *As he was moving away, he told me to take care of you and her.*

Who is this her, anyway? He mentioned her to me, too.

"Mister Bryn!" shouted a human girl as she ran out of the tall grass. "Mister Bryn, you must see this! There's an egg!"

Chapter 41

It was raining. Rulsaesan knew that this was different than the normal rainstorm; it had come out of nowhere, and it only extended to the beginning of the forest. That, combined with the pain she was currently feeling, worried her greatly. Something was wrong; she worried that she'd either have to help Jena cope with Bryn's death or keep Teltresan from dying after the death of her mate.

What is wrong, Rulsaesan? Deyraeno asked as he flew out of the entrance and walked up to her.

The Child of Light shuddered. *I do not know. It feels as if there was a terrible death just a few minutes ago. I'm frightened.*

Delbralfi is feeling much better. He was walking around before I came up here.

And Jena? How is she?

She is fine, Rulsaesan. Perhaps you are just imagining things, and the death you sensed was The Fire Queen's death.

I did not sense her death! Rulsaesan screamed. Then, seeing the hurt in her mate's eyes, she said, *I am sorry, Dey. It couldn't be her death; this loss was felt by all who witnessed it, and a great amount of love is now coming from the dead instead of the living. I could try to use my powers tonight when they are dreaming to learn what happened, but for now I can only wait for the news to come.*

We will wait together, Deyraeno said as he grasped her tail. After a few moments, he squinted and asked, *What is that?*

Rulsaesan squinted and stared at the large moving object Deyraeno was looking at. After a few seconds, she recognized the figure and grinned with relief. *Iden! You have returned! I'm so glad you-*

Iden stopped dancing and spun around to face them. He smiled grimly as he walked over to them, his wings unfurled from the last movement in his dance.

Rulsaesan froze and screamed in horror. Iden was not gaining strength from the rain anymore; the rain was falling through him. Rulsaesan could see through him to the Watchzard rock he had made his own. His eyes were the only thing that still seemed alive, and they were not even the same as they were before. They had changed from lavender to the deep shade of brown that he had in his youth before he had felt the pain of love unreturned.

Deyraeno began sobbing. *No, Iden, please tell me you aren't-*

Incapable of physical form anymore? Sorry, I can't tell you that, Dey, Iden said. *But don't worry about me; I'm fine. I get to leave this world dancing in the rain and happy; not many can say that.*

Iden, you were one of my greatest and truest friends, Rulsaesan said, holding back tears of her own. *Please don't forget us when you go to the stars.*

Who said anything about becoming a star? Iden asked, sounding almost hurt. *Why would I become a star, when I could not watch over you two when the rain falls?*

What do you mean, you won't become a star? Rulsaesan asked, terrified for her friend. *What will you be, the rain itself?*

Yes. I will be with you when the rain falls, and there will never be a drought, Iden said as began to fade away. *Don't worry; I will go to the stars someday. But for now, I have too many that I care about still on this earth to leave it entirely. You will be fine, as long as you love each other with complete devotion. It is what He wants for you, and it is what I want as well.*

He? Rulsaesan asked.

The Lord of the Sky, of course, Idenno said. *He is wonderful, Rulsaesan.*

Then I could accept no less of myself, Rulsaesan whispered.

Goodbye for now, my friends, the former Watchzard said, each word softer than the word before, until there was nothing but the rain.

Rulsaesan lost all composure and began crying on Dey's shoulder. Not even his embrace could fully comfort her, for she could sense that he was just as upset as she was.

I cannot claim to love you as much as he did, Dey said. *I fear it is a standard that I will never be able to meet, even though I do love you very much.*

No one can love as much as Iden did, Dey, Rulsaesan said. *It is an ideal no one should try to meet. But that does not mean I will not love you as fully and truly as I can. If we do that until our dying days, we will truly honor his memory and the sacrifices he made for us.*

Chapter 42

Xolt and Bryn walked through the tall grass until they saw the egg that Delma had found. The egg was as tall as Bryn, and it looked as if it had been left alone unexpectedly, for it was on its side and caught in a patch of tall grass. Despite this, the dark tan egg did not have any cracks or signs of damage.

"What kind of egg is it?" Delma asked. "It's huge!"

"I don't know," Bryn said quietly. "We should probably let the Onizards talk about it, though."

"You think I'm too little to understand what's going on," Delma said with a frown.

"I think this is a private matter," Bryn said. "I'm going to be leaving them alone as well. Come, let's go try to find some food. Preferably food that doesn't make me think a tree is Jena."

"I am hungry," Delma said as she giggled at the tree comment and followed Bryn toward the forest.

When the humans were gone, Deldenno said, *A tree is Jena? What happened to him?*

It's a long story, Xolt said. *Something you probably don't want to hear right now when there's serious business to discuss. Where did the egg come from?*

I do not know, Deldenno sighed. *So, do we think it's an Onizard egg?*

I think it is, Xolt said. *But how did it get here?*

The screaming, Ransenna said. *There was often screaming at night, and when Idenno died, the Fire Queen started screaming about a lost father.*

That wasn't like the Fire Queen, Deldenno said. *She's never cared about anyone other than herself. What was it about Idenno that made her do that?*

I don't know, Xolt said, fighting his tears at this reference to Idenno as something that was gone. He was not a child anymore; he was not supposed to cry.

You don't suppose it's his egg, do you? Ransenna asked Deldenno.

I am certain Uncle Iden would not have told us if that had happened, Deldenno said. *He was always trying to protect me; this egg is probably a result of his protection.*

Then we must protect her, Ransenna said.

Deldenno turned to Ransenna and attempted to smile. *We must. He asked us both to take care of her. Part of that would have to be hiding her parentage from the rest of the Sandleyr.*

And hide the full nature of Idenno's sacrifice? Ransenna asked, her eyes widening. *How could you suggest that, Deldenno? What if her mother returns?*

She won't know the egg survived. She can think that this is our daughter, Deldenno said, blushing as he seemed to be thinking of the effect this would have on the Sandleyr's view of their relationship. *I was hoping that we'd survive and one day have a child together, and I guess we can have that dream. That is, if you'd agree to do this.*

Be your joinmate, you mean? Ransenna asked as she turned toward him. From the look in her eyes, Xolt could tell that she agreed to the idea.

Well, yes, Deldenno said as he stared at the ground. *I would not suggest it if I didn't have the deepest feelings of respect and love for you. I wish the circumstances were different and that we'd have more time to properly court each other, but…would you be my joinmate and the mother of my child?*

I will, Delden, Ransenna said as she picked up the egg and rocked it. Then, after a quiet moment, she began to laugh.

What is it? Deldenno asked.

Delculble will say I'm going far too fast.

Bral is going to want to kill me when he finds out about the egg, Deldenno said. *But he doesn't have to know that she isn't ours. No one does,* he added as he turned to Xolt. *You must swear not to tell anyone. If you have to tell your Bond anything, tell Bryn that the egg was actually ours, but we didn't want to admit it in front of the girl. I don't want this child to grow up thinking she was the abandoned child of the Fire Queen, the result of the rape of an innocent Onizard she killed. Your father grew up like that, Xolt, and it nearly killed him from the guilt of it. My daughter is not going to live like that.*

Our daughter, Ransenna said, smiling as she corrected him. *Our daughter will grow up with love.*

Xolt smiled. It seemed that even as a good Onizard died, two good Onizards had found comfort in each other. *I swear that I will not tell him. I will keep the secret for you, and for Idenno.*

Chapter 43

We're home! Xolt exclaimed as he landed safely, looking at the familiar sights of the Sandleyr. Several Onizards had appeared on their ledges, cheering for their arrival. Bryn did not really care about them; he had more important people to see.

Bryn stepped off Xolt's tail onto the floor of the Invitation Hall. As one numb from a long journey, he walked toward his leyr.

"Mister Bryn!" Delma exclaimed.

Bryn winced and turned around. The girl had become his friend, but she was delaying him even more. "What is it, Delma?"

The girl stared at the ground for a moment before asking, "I was wondering if maybe you and Miss Jena can be sorta like my parents now that my parents are gone."

Bryn smiled. "I suppose we can. I'll have to ask Jena, though."

"Of course we can," Jena said as she stepped out of the leyr.

Bryn gasped. Though her beauty had not changed since he left, it seemed that her beauty was rarer and more beautiful after dealing with such a long journey. Now, both Onizards and humans had died to make their love last longer in the land of the living. It was an overwhelming thing to think about, and it put a great responsibility on the Zarders.

Bryn wanted to tell Jena how much he loved her. He wanted to say that in the moment when he thought he was going to die, he had no other thoughts but thoughts of her. He wanted to let her know how much he cared about her, how he hoped to be a good father to her child. But all he could do was sob and say, "Idenno is dead. We failed."

Jena pulled him close to her and held him as he cried on her shoulder. "I know. Rulsaesan told me. But you did not fail, Bryn. You came back to me."

You did not fail, Bryn, Rulsaesan said as she and Deyraeno walked toward the gathering group. *You left on a quest to free the hostages. Now they are all free.*

Iden is in a better place now, Deyraeno said. His voice was calm, but Bryn could see that he and his joinmate were both stressed from grief. Their skin was paler than it was when he had left, and their eyes were swollen as if they had both been crying for a long time.

He is happy now; that is the most important thing, Rulsaesan said. *He feels no more pain.*

Where is my father? Xolt asked.

I'm here, Xoltorble, Delbralfi said as he walked toward the group.

Father! Xolt shouted as he ran toward the Child of Fire and embraced him. *I missed you.*

I missed you too, my son, Delbralfi said.

Xolt! Erfasfi exclaimed as he ran to greet his brother. *We all missed you so much. You need to tell us all about your adventures.*

"I claim the tree story," Bryn said quickly.

No fair! Xolt protested. *That was the funniest part of the journey.*

"Tree story?" Jena asked, her eyes narrowing as she smirked. "This sounds intriguing."

"It's a story for a different day," Bryn said. "For now, we must rest and think of those who could not return."

Yes, Rulsaesan said. *Let us all rest and rejoice, for the heroes of the Sandleyr have returned.*

The true hero has not, Xolt said, hanging his head in shame.

Of course he has returned. Rulsaesan said. *As long as the rain falls and our memories remain strong, he will never leave.*

Chapter 44

Delma shivered as she sat on the Watchzard rock and watched the rain fall around her. It had rained so often in the past month, and the Blueflower tree she had planted by the Watchzard rock in Idenno's memory was prospering. Though she had not known him, the way his death affected her new friends upset her greatly. It was clear from the way Xolt was shying away from the world that he was depressed. Somehow she doubted that Idenno wanted Xolt to feel that way. Even though she had never seen him in life, from the way everyone talked about him, he was a very special Onizard indeed.

Her song about her parents was slowly getting better. Delma experimentally sang a few notes before she decided they would not fit well with the rest of the song. She would get it right with practice; she was sure Mister Bryn and Miss Jena would help her get it right. Maybe the new children, both human and Onizard, would listen when it was finished.

As she looked about, she thought for a moment that she saw the form of a Child of Water dancing about. But when she blinked, the smiling Onizard had disappeared.

The egg is hatching! Deldenno shouted as he took off from the tall structure that they called the Leyr Grounds.

The egg! So much hope had been placed in that egg. From the way Deldenno and Ransenna had been acting since she found that egg, it seemed that they were hoping for some reincarnation of Idenno instead of a unique individual Onizard. Delma wasn't quite sure that was fair to the new baby. The pressure to live up to the ideal of Idenno would be a heavy burden on her, and he wasn't even her father!

Or him, Delma reminded herself. The hatchling could just as easily be a boy. No one seemed to think it was a boy, but she didn't want to offend him if he was a boy.

Delma, Deldenno said as he landed by the Watchzard rock, *you're Invited.*

"Invited? What does that mean?"

It means you're supposed to watch the egg hatch with us, Deldenno said.

"Really? I would be honored, Mister Delden."

Come, climb onto my tail and I will take you up there.

Delma obeyed, but she paused for a moment as she thought she saw the strange Child of Water again. This was just getting too weird. Since when did Onizards have the power to disappear and reappear at will?

Deldenno carried her to the top of the towering structure, over the bowl shape at the top. Ransenna was waiting there for them, her eyes focused on the rocking egg. As Deldenno set her down, Delma watched as the egg rocked one final time before the hatchling Onizard tumbled out of the egg.

She was a Child of Earth, and she was beautiful. Truly, she was not the most graceful of Onizards, for she stumbled a few times before getting up, but Delma saw that she had an inner beauty waiting to blossom. Her skin was dark green, and the sinews of her wings were the color of fresh grass. She slowly opened her eyes, revealing that they were dark brown and shaped much like the eyes of Idenno were in the carving Deldenno made in the Watchzard rock. It was so strange to think that she wasn't even related to him.

There was no way she could possibly be the daughter of Idenno, though. Delma could see that from the way Ransenna and Deldenno looked at her, their eyes glimmering with love and devotion. The hatchling's eyes were the color of Ransenna's eyes, and if her skin changed color to blue, it would be the same hue as Deldenno's skin. They were her parents, and no little girl could be luckier.

Delma? A new voice said as it entered her head.

Suddenly, part of Delma's mind was in the mind of the hatchling. She could feel the terror, as if she were worried that somehow she would not live up to the standards set before her.

Am I a good Bond, Delma? the hatchling asked, her voice trembling.

"A very good Bond," Delma said as she ran up to the hatchling and hugged her. Then, once she realized that the elder Onizards were watching in awe, she smiled and said. "I'd like you to meet the only Onizard who is little like me. Her name is Amblomna. But then, you already knew that."

Actually, I didn't, Deldenno said as he looked toward the rain clouds that were lazily drifting toward the sea. *Sometimes it is good to be surprised.*

Inhabitants of the Sandleyr

The Ones in the Wilderness

Bryn is the second Zarder, and the husband of Jena. No one can doubt his loyalty to his wife.

Xoltorble is Bryn's Bond and the son of Teltresan and Delbralfi. He is not quite mature yet, though he is ready to prove his abilities by saving the Fire Queen's hostages.

Delma is a ten year old girl who found her way to the Sandleyr after the tragic destruction of her village. She may be the key to finding the Fire Queen and rescuing the missing Onizards.

Idenno is the former Watchzard of the Sandleyr. Though Rulsaesan officially retired him from that duty, he has still been keeping his eye out for the Fire Queen. Unfortunately, he is not the kind of fighter that the Fire Queen is.

Deldenno is a son of Rulsaesan and Deyraeno and Bond of Delbralfi. He was named for the Watchzard Idenno, a friend of his parents. When he was captured, Idenno did everything in his power to protect him.

Ransenna is an Onizard who owes her life to Jena after the rescue of her Bond, Delculble. She seems to be a no-nonsense Child of Earth, but there is more to her than first appearances would suggest.

Deybralfi, the Fire Queen, was banished from the Sandleyr six years ago after Senraeno and Teltresan defeated her. She has a serious grudge against Senraeno and all Children of Light, especially Rulsaesan.

The Day Kingdom

Leyrque Rulsaesan is the beloved ruler of the Day Kingdom. The woman who was once weakened by the lack of another Child of Light has proven to be a strong and just ruler.

Lady Teltresan is the youngest Child of Light. A former non-nature, she gained her powers after courageously standing up to the Fire Queen.

Deyraeno is the mate of Lady Rulsaesan, and a protective father.

Delbralfi is the proud joinmate of Lady Teltresan. He is the only Onizard to be the mate of a Child of Light and the child of two Children of Light (Mekanni and Delsenni).

Delculble is a son of Rulsaesan and Deyraeno and Bond of Ransenna. The only dramatic thing to happen to this Onizard was his near-drowning at birth. Since Zarder Jena saved his life, he feels indebted to her.

Erfasfi is the son of Teltresan and Delbralfi, and the twin brother of Xoltorble. His immaturity leaves much to be desired, but he has a good heart.

Amsaena and Rulraeno are the daughters of Rulsaesan and Deyraeno. While they have not led as interesting a life as their siblings, they are by no means less loved by their parents.

Ammasan is the deceased ruler of the Day Kingdom. After the Fire Queen murdered her, no one inherited her powers for ten years.

Ranbralfi was the mate of Ammasan and the father of the Fire Queen.

The Night Kingdom

Leyrkan Mekanni rules the Night Kingdom with his joinmate, Lady Delsenni. Mekanni has struggled with an illness that frightens many away from his kingdom, but being a grandfather has made him a happier Onizard.

Lady Delsenni rules the Night Kingdom with her joinmate, Leyrkan Mekanni. She took on the role of protector and nurturer for Jena and Senraeno when they were in trouble, and now enjoys being a grandmother.

Jena is the first human to become the Bond of an Onizard. She tries to lead a normal life in spite of her newfound celebrity.

Senraeno is a son of Rulsaesan and Deyraeno and the Bond of Jena. His strong sense of justice is tempered by a strong heart.

Senmani was the mother of Mekanni and Idenno and the ruler of the Night Kingdom. The Fire Queen murdered her and Ammasan.

Liked what you read?

Read on for an excerpt from
The Blood of Senbralni

But I can see that Amblomna is not ready. I swore to protect you and your family, but I cannot sacrifice myself again.

And I could not sacrifice my best friend's daughter without a valid reason, Rulsaesan said as she looked up at him.

The ghost in the rain partially vanished, as if her words had nearly shocked him out of existence. *I had hoped no one would guess that truth, but I should have known that you'd learn eventually.*

She has your eyes, Iden, Rulsaesan said. *When I first learned that I was having a grandchild, I expected that she would look like my child and his mate. Instead, I saw a beautiful girl who looks much like you and Ammasan. I feared that my best friend was hiding his pain at the end of his life, but when I saw Amblomna for the first time, I knew...and it hurt me to know it. It was like a sudden reminder that my best friend and mentor are dead.*

Please don't hate her for her bloodline, Idenno said. *She is more than that.*

I know, Rulsaesan said. *I have always known that bloodline means little when it comes to a person's character. Besides, though I knew the day that she hatched that I was not looking at my blood descendant, that does not change the fact that she is my granddaughter. She is the last connection that Deyraeno and I have to you and Ammasan; how could I not love her?*

But you just said she was a reminder of our deaths.

It was only for a moment, and it did no damage, Rulsaesan smiled. *Occasionally something she does reminds me of you or Ammasan, but the memory is not as bittersweet now. I am glad a good Onizard will carry your legacy.*

If you are counting on Amblomna to carry my legacy, why did you help her risk her life?

Because that is part of your legacy, Rulsaesan said. *You flew to your death without hesitation, because of love. Now, Amby thinks she's doing the same thing for love.*

You really think she has a chance? Idenno asked. *I couldn't defeat the Fire Queen, and I was capable of exploiting her weakness to water.*

One weakness, Rulsaesan said. *The Fire Queen has more than one weakness. I have been in her dreams.*

Her weakness is her dreams?

No, Rulsaesan said. *Her weakness is Amblomna. She thinks that her daughter is dead. With the right persuasion, the Fire Queen would probably do anything for her long-lost daughter.*

Or she could kill Amblomna before finding out about their connection, Idenno said. *I've heard her wailing about my demise and about her father's death, but that doesn't do either of us any good.*

It is a risk, but it is a risk that we must take, Rulsaesan said. *Iden, the plan's success relies on Amblomna knowing of this weakness.*

Why haven't you told her, then? Idenno asked. *If you're basing the plan on that, you might as well let Amby know what you think she needs to know.*

She is not my daughter, Rulsaesan said. *That is Ransenna or Deldenno's job, possibly even your job, but not mine. She deserves to know the truth, but not from me. I do not even know the full tale.*

There is not much to tell, Idenno said. *And what story there is would harm her almost as badly as the Fire Queen could. You were not there; you were not…violated. You do not know what it is like to have a daughter that you love in spite of that, a daughter you can only speak to in the fleeting moments when she decides to go outside when it's raining.*

You are right; I do not, Rulsaesan said. *But you do not know what it is like to have to make the most terrible decision of your life, when each path brings pain and suffering to your loved ones, and even your best intentions may betray you in the end.*

You are wrong, Idenno said as he stepped off the Watchzard Rock. *I made that decision the day I chose to die for you and your family. The day I chose to prove my love for you one last time.*

Rulsaesan sighed and bowed her head. *Sometimes I wish you didn't tell me these things, Idenno.*

Yet you ask me to tell harsher truths to my only daughter, Idenno said as glanced up at the quickly brightening sky. *I must go now. I need time to think.*

You aren't bound by time anymore, Iden; why do you need time to think?

It is more for you than for me, he said.

Then the sun was shining over the Sandleyr, and Rulsaesan felt utterly alone. She was glad that it was over, but at the same time, she worried about the effect of her decision. Amblomna had to return to the Sandleyr, but she also had to confront the demon. There was no stepping off that path, even if Idenno thought there was a way.

Sara Jo Easton drew the first Onizards when she was bored in math class (in her defense, it was the second day in a row of graphing a plane). Over a decade later, she has attended college for journalism and now lives with her two insane cats. Times have changed, but she would still get bored in a math class, especially if it involved two days in a row of graphing planes.

Contact the Author at:
Blog: http://thesandleyr.blogspot.com
Twitter: http://twitter.com/SaraJoEaston
Facebook:
http://facebook.com/AuthorSaraJoEaston
E-mail: zardermail@gmail.com